Half-Court Trap

Kevin heronJones

James Lorimer & Company Ltd., Publishers
Toronto

James Lorimer & Company Ltd., Publishers acknowledges funding support from
the Ontario Arts Council (OAC), an agency of the Government of Ontario. We
acknowledge the support of the Canada Council for the Arts, which last year
invested $153 million to bring the arts to Canadians throughout the country.
This project has been made possible in part by the Government of Canada and
with the support of Ontario Creates.

Cover design: Tyler Cleroux
Cover image: iStock

Library and Archives Canada Cataloguing in Publication (Paperback)

Title: Half-court trap / Kevin heronJones.
Names: heronJones, Kevin, 1975- author.
Series: Sports stories.
Description: Series statement: Sports stories
Identifiers: Canadiana (print) 20210210575 | Canadiana (ebook) 20210210605
    | ISBN 9781459416444 (softcover) | ISBN 9781459416451 (EPUB)
Classification: LCC PS8615.I754 H34 2021 | DDC jC813/.6—dc23

Published by:
James Lorimer &
Company Ltd., Publishers
117 Peter Street, Suite 304
Toronto, ON, Canada
M5V 0M3
www.lorimer.ca

Distributed in Canada by:
Formac Lorimer Books
5502 Atlantic Street
Halifax, NS, Canada
B3H 1G4

Distributed in the US by:
Lerner Publisher Services
241 1st Ave. N.
Minneapolis, MN, USA
55401
www.lernerbooks.com

Printed and bound in Canada.
Manufactured by Friesens Corporation in Altona, Manitoba,
Canada in June 2021.
Job #277237

This novel is dedicated to my son Tyce. Continue to believe in yourself and strive to see your miracles manifest.

To all youth athletic players who are learning to play the game of life while learning to play the sports they love.

Contents

1 Down by ONE

Both players wrestled for the rebound. Each gripped it with two hands, trying to rip it away from the other, when the referee blew the whistle. *Tweeeet!* Although the play was over, the boys kept grappling for control of the ball. The referee blew his whistle again. *Tweeeet. Tweeeet!* He blew it two, three, four more times as he raced over to separate the boys locked in combat. Finally, Nigel let go of the ball and pushed it into the number five on the chest of his opponent.

Nigel stormed to the bench where Coach Shabaka was waiting. The boy left holding the ball lost his balance and fell to the floor.

"Nigel, you know better. On this team, we don't do that," said Coach Shabaka as Nigel plopped down and slammed his fist on the bench.

"But, Coach —" Nigel pleaded.

"But nothing. That's how you get kicked out of the game. On the Power, we don't fight, you understand?"

"But, Coach Shabaka, he started it."

"Ya, Coach, they started it," a few of the other boys chimed in, walking off the court toward the bench.

"I don't care who started it. Boys, it ends now," said their coach. "I've taught you guys to be tough, to play tough. But it doesn't mean you fight."

Nigel shuffled his feet in anger. His eyes were glossy with rage. "But, Coach, he called me fat!"

"Who called you fat?" asked Coach Shabaka.

Nigel jumped to his feet, pointing in the direction of the opponent's bench.

"Number 5. He been calling me 'fat-boy baller' all game!" Nigel said.

"Ya, Coach, the Tigers have been calling us names," said Asim. He was bent over, trying to catch his breath. "They . . . they say that we suck. That we should be playing in the girls' league."

"Really?! Girls' league? I'm sure the girls from my daughter's team could tear all you apart on the court," said Coach Shabaka.

"They talk a lot of trash, Coach, and Number 5 goes to my school," said Sundeep from the bench. "He's always getting in fights."

"Okay, boys, I get it," said Coach Shabaka. "I'll have a talk with their coach. In the meantime, I need you to stay focused on the game. This is summer league playoffs. There's no next week if we don't win today. So don't let these boys get under your skin. We're down eleven points. We can get that back. Let's finish the quarter strong. Let's pull out this win and play in the championship."

The boys huddled closer together as Coach Shabaka gave further instruction.

"Nigel, you and Kash run that pick and roll again. Everyone else spread the floor. Rebound when the shot goes up. Make sure you are sliding your feet on defence. Keep your hands up, ready to poke that ball out when they show it. We got this, guys. We got this! Hands in. Power on three. One, two, three!"

The boys extended their hands to the middle of the huddle, stacking one on top of the other and hollered as loud as they could. "POWER!"

Kash and Nigel did just as Coach Shabaka told them. Nigel was patient, crossing the ball left to right like a hypnotist as Number 5 guarded him. A slight head nod signalled Kash to run up and stand against Number 5's left shoulder, preventing him from following Nigel. Number 5 crashed into Kash's chest, freeing Nigel to dribble to his right and score easily. Nigel gave Number 5 a look that said, *Ya, you can't guard me* while running backward, getting ready to play defence. The Power were down nine points now, with five minutes left in the game.

Number 11 brought the ball up the court for the Tigers, waiting for his teammates to get in place. They spread the court as Number 5 cut through the middle of the defence to receive the pass. Nigel tried to follow, but was a step behind. Number 5 had an open layup when Kash flew in from behind, blocking the shot off the backboard. The ball ricocheted to half court. Nigel chased after it and quickly scooped up the pumpkin. He scored easily on a breakaway. The Power were down by seven points. They continued to play with discipline, and were able to cut the score to three with just two minutes left on the clock.

Feeling extra confident, the Power forced the Tigers to throw up a difficult shot that clanked off the side of the rim. Asim grabbed the rebound and ran the ball up the court, looking for an easy score. However, the Tigers got back on time.

The Power set up their offence, every player getting in place. Nigel set a pick for Asim and rolled toward the basket, his hand up, looking for the pass. Nigel caught the pass near the baseline and two players ran toward him. Nigel was trapped. He had to shoot a difficult shot from behind the backboard or get rid of the ball before the Tigers surrounded him. Then Nigel noticed Asim wide open under the basket. He bounced a pass under Number 5's hand to Asim for an uncontested score. The Power were down one with less than a minute on the clock.

The Power set up a full-court press, guarding the Tigers' players on both sides of the court as the Tigers tried to inbound the ball. The referee began his count, as Number 5 searched for a teammate to catch the inbound pass. One-two-three-four the referee counted on his hand with fingers high in the air. If he counted to five, it would result in a turnover and it would be the Power's ball. Number 5 quickly vaulted a pass forward to his Number 11, who was cutting down the sideline. Number 11 fumbled the pass, and struggled to get control of the ball and dribble at the same time.

Coach Shabaka was yelling at the Power players, "Foul him. Foul him!" Nigel charged in and stole the ball with only nine seconds left on the clock. Nigel knew he was going to win the game for the Power. He dribbled as fast as he could through and around Tiger defenders, as if they were pylons in practice. Only one defender stood between him and the game-winning layup. Number 5 stood in his defensive stance, waiting for Nigel to drive.

I'll show him who's fat, Nigel thought as he got closer to the basket. *He wants to mess with me! I'm gonna mess him up and win the game at the same time.* All his self-talk caused Nigel to become confused. He couldn't decide whether to lay the ball up or take a jumpshot for the win. The confusion stunted his jump. He had no lift. He ended up floating something between a shot and a layup. He watched the ball as it left his hands, and hoped that it would drop through the net.

Nigel's indecision prompted Number 5 to swoop in and gobble up the shot with one hand. *Blaaap!*

He slapped the ball back into Nigel's face. Nigel fell to the ground. Number 5 stood above him, wagging his index finger, saying, "Not today. No, no sir. Not today, fat-boy baller."

Nigel watched Number 5 turn to his teammates, laughing. "Can you believe Chubs over here? If he dropped a few pounds, he might be able to jump a little higher next time. Somebody get this guy a stretcher, cuz he too heavy to even pick himself up."

2 Good SPORTSMANSHIP

The Tigers surrounded Number 5 and jumped in a circle of celebration. The Power hung their heads with disappointment and slowly walked back to the bench. Nigel stayed on the floor, lying on his back with his eyes closed. He couldn't believe he missed the shot. He couldn't believe he let Number 5 get in his way.

Coach Shabaka praised the boys for their effort. "Don't hang your heads, boys. You gave yourselves the chance to win. It just didn't go our way today. It's okay. I'm proud of you."

Nigel picked himself off the floor and straggled to the Power huddle just in time to hear Coach Shabaka say, "All right, boys. Let's go shake hands. Power on three."

Coach Shabaka threw his hand to the middle. All the boys followed, except Nigel, who was watching the Tigers celebrate. Coach Shabaka hollered out to him, "Nigel! Nigel, you with us?"

Startled, Nigel threw his hand to the middle, atop all the other players' hands.

Coach Shabaka continued with his count. "One, two, three! POWER!"

"Power," the boys repeated, with much less excitement than their coach.

The boys dragged themselves to mid-court where the Tigers were already lined up to shake hands. Nigel was the last in line. Coach Shabaka joined the line behind him. The line moved forward, as the boys held their hands out to slap the hands of the other team walking by.

"G.G. Good game. G.G.," the boys repeated as they smacked each hand.

Nigel had no intention of shaking hands with the opposing team. *These guys are punks*, Nigel thought. *They ain't got no honour. They ain't showed good sportsmanship, so why should I?* When the first Tigers player in line got to Nigel, he looked back, confused. The second and third boys in line for the Tigers looked back the same way after passing Nigel, who had not slapped hands with them. Nigel just walked by with his hand in his pocket. He smiled at their reaction, until he felt a tap on his shoulder.

"C'mon, Nigel. You know better. Shake hands," said Coach Shabaka.

Nigel reluctantly raised his hand and connected with the rest of the boys who passed through the line. When Number 5 reached Nigel, he slapped Nigel's hand extra hard. The two boys stared angrily as they passed each other.

Coach Shabaka gathered the Power together for a

last word before releasing them to their parents. "Boys, enjoy the rest of your summer. I'll see many of you in a few weeks for fall ball. Keep practising. Every day. Dribble and shoot as much as you can. Anywhere. If it's raining and you can't go outside, then dribble in your garage or your basement. If you don't have a rim at home, shoot at a spot against the wall. Just keep getting better. All right, guys?"

The boys held their backpacks and water bottles as if carrying luggage as they listened to Coach Shabaka continue. "And, boys, be proud of yourselves. We've had a tremendous season. All of you, practise your favourite move or shot over and over and over, until you do it so well that no one can stop you when you do it. All right? Your parents are waiting. Let's go."

Water bottles and backpacks bounced off legs as the boys ran to where their parents were grouped together. Nigel was last, and walked slowly as Coach Shabaka followed. Parents waved and thanked Coach Shabaka, ushering their sons to the exit. A few remained behind to shake Coach Shabaka's hand and chat.

Nigel's father waited until all the other parents were gone before approaching Coach Shabaka. Nigel was getting hugs from his mom and little brother.

"Hey, Coach," said Nigel's father. "Tough game today, eh?"

"Sure was," Coach Shabaka replied. "I thought Nigel was gonna put us over the top at the buzzer.

Man. Wasn't meant to be. But the boys played hard. That's all I could ask. They did well. Especially since we fell behind early."

"You did a good job with them, Coach. We almost had the comeback. It looked pretty heated out there. Thought there was gonna be a fight."

"Ya, y'know what? The boys were complaining that the other team were calling them names and teasing them throughout the game. Nigel said one of the boys kept calling him fat." Nigel's ears perked up as he heard Coach Shabaka mention fat. "I had to calm Nigel down a number of times. He didn't like the boys talking about his weight and was ready to throw down. Your boy is hot-blooded. Can go from zero to a hundred real quick."

"Yes, yes. Nigel does have a temper. We talk to him about it all the time," said Nigel's father.

Nigel shook his head, thinking, *I wouldn't have a temper if those guys didn't make me mad!*

Nigel's father continued, "And we've been trying to get him to lose some weight. He needs to lose some weight. It will help his game."

Nigel was shocked to hear his father tell the coach that he needed to lose weight. He was used to hearing it at home. But he felt betrayed that his father would embarrass him outside too. *How could he say that in front of Coach?* he wondered. *And act like I'm not here listening.*

Coach Shabaka replied, "I don't think Nigel is fat, by any means. He's stocky, sure, but he's in excellent shape. He's one of the fastest kids on the team, and has great endurance. His size helps him get to wherever he wants to on the court, like Zion Williamson or Charles Barkley."

Thanks, Coach, Nigel thought, happy that Coach Shabaka was on his side.

"Sure, but he could still lose some weight," Nigel's father said. "I'm going to get him on a strict regimen, then you'll see."

OMG nooooooo! Nigel thought. He looked up at Coach Shabaka for sympathy.

"Nigel, you had a great game," Coach Shabaka said, holding out his fist. "You were the leading scorer again. Don't worry about the loss. Enjoy the rest of your summer, okay? I'll try to get you on my squad again for fall ball. You just keep improving that jumpshot."

Nigel pounded his fist against Coach Shabaka's and thanked him, noticing Number 5 across the court high-fiving what were obviously his parents, brothers and sister. Nigel swore that he was going to make Number 5 pay for calling him heavy and teasing him on the court. He wasn't sure how yet, but he knew Number 5 was going to pay.

3 Mini REVENGE

Nigel was practising with Coach Shabaka's daughter Kiya, waiting for the Brampton fall ball pre-draft workout to begin. Nigel and Kiya went to the same school. They spent a lot of time practising and playing one-on-one after games and practices.

"So, Key, lemme tell you," said Nigel. "This season, I'm not holding anything back. The way we went out during summer league, it don't sit good with me, yo. I'm gonna rock this league, you feel me?"

"Ya, Dad told me how close you guys were to winning. Sucks, man," Kiya said.

"Ya. And, yo, the thing that gets me most is all the trash they kept talking. Especially this one fool, Number 5. Ah, man. If he was here today, yo, I would kick his . . . y'know what I'm sayin'. Anyway, this season's gonna be different. I guarantee."

"It better be, Nige. Cuz if you plan to catch up to me, you gonna need a few more trophies. You just need to play free, like when you and I play. Don't let clowns get under your skin, y'know. It takes you off your game."

"Ya, I guess. When you and I play, it's more fun. When I play in the league, it's a different story."

"Nigel, how long we been playing together? Like, two and half, three years? Have you not learned anything! You always complaining about someone on the court. So-and-so did this or that to you. You care too much about what other people think of you. Look how many times girls try to fight with me on the court. I don't let them bother me. They can say what they want. At the end of the day, I'm gonna take their heart on the court and win. That's it. You gotta let your game do the talking."

"True. I gotta practise more, like you do. You dribble your ball everywhere. Even if you're just walking to the corner store. You even sleep with your ball."

"I love the game, dude. They gonna bury me with my ball. Like, right in the casket beside me." Kiya laughed. "Nige, you're like my brother, yo. I hate to see you this way. Listen, Dad always tells me this. Respect the game, respect yourself and everything else will take care of itself."

"Key, you tryin' to rap now. Better stick to basketball." Nigel laughed.

"Please. I'll outrhyme you and outplay you at the same time. And you know that's true!"

Nigel nodded in agreement. Kiya grabbed the rebound after Nigel missed a turnaround jumpshot and tossed the red, black and green ball back in his direction.

"Yo, Nige, be easy, we'll link up. I gotta go. Remember, let your game do the talking. See ya later."

Nigel waved bye to Kiya as she jogged off. He kept shooting. *She's right. I've gotta ignore those guys. I just hate it when they talk all that fat stuff. Besides, I'm not really fat. I'm just kinda big? I guess if I was slimmer, then no one could tell me nothing. If I was slimmer, I'd have no problems.*

The whistles blew and the trainers gathered the boys together to start running exercises. Nigel noticed Coach Shabaka on the sideline, chewing on the end of his pencil as he watched the boys running layup drills from the sideline of the court. They nodded at each other as Nigel jogged to the back of the line. Nigel had been playing for Coach Shabaka for a couple of years. He hadn't started out as the best player, but he worked hard, practised every day and followed the coach's instructions. Now he was one of the most skilled players on the Power.

Nigel knew that Coach Shabaka would try to get as many of the boys from the summer league team on this team as he could. Nigel hoped that he'd be able to play with his boys Omari and Kash again. Together, they could possibly win a championship this season. As the boys switched from layups to jumpshots, Nigel wondered how many potential new players would fit in with the Power. They had to be speedy, lock-down defenders, who could force turnovers and fast breaks for easy baskets. Boys who weren't afraid to hustle and work hard. Boys like Nigel.

As Nigel re-entered the line, he looked around the gym at all the kids running drills. The gym was packed with players. He looked around at his competition, thinking that he and the Power were going to have an excellent chance at the championship this year.

TWEEET! The lead trainer blew the whistle and all the boys stopped suddenly. He stood in the middle of the gym and spoke loud enough for all the players to hear.

"All right, boys. We want to see some of your one-on-one skills. So, in this drill, we want the boys in the rebounding line to now play defence. Okay! So, meet your opponent at half court, shadow him and prevent him from scoring. You got that? Boys with the ball, dribble as fast as you can and score. You only get one shot. If the defender steals the ball or blocks your shot, go off to the side and do twenty push-ups."

A low murmur began as the boys looked around the gym at one another.

"All right!" the lead trainer yelled, clapping his hands. "Let's go! Don't just stand there. Let's get it!"

The boys jumped, as if startled by firecrackers, and began the drill. Nigel was in the offence line, watching as other boys missed layups and jumpshots or turned the ball over repeatedly. The sidelines were filling up with boys paying their push-up punishments. Nigel knew he would not be one of them. He was thinking about the moves he was going to make, when one of the boys threw a ball in his direction. Without taking note who his defender was, Nigel sped forward, dribbling at top speed. As he approached half court, he saw who was defending him — Tigers Number 5. When Nigel realized who it was, he dribbled even harder and faster. This time there was no self-talk. Nigel knew exactly what he was going to do.

Number 5 tried to shuffle his feet to stay in front. But Nigel powered forward like a steaming locomotive and launched like a rocket, his knee directed at Number 5's gut. Number 5's body was too slender to absorb the blow. He collapsed like an umbrella and crashed to the floor, while Nigel finished with a made layup. Huffing and puffing heavily, Nigel scowled at Number 5 as he joined the defensive line. He dared Number 5 to make eye contact, but Number 5 just got up and brushed himself off. Nigel was surprised that he was doing the intimidating himself. That he could outmuscle Number 5 on the court. Still mean mugging on the outside, Nigel smiled on the inside, proud that he had gotten the better of Number 5 this time. But Nigel wasn't satisfied yet. He still had something up his sleeve for Number 5 if he ever got him alone.

4 Draft DAY

Nigel stared at the LeBron James poster on the wall in his bedroom. He tried to mimic LeBron's pose, flexing both muscular arms with his shirt off. Nigel carried the pose to his mirror and examined his pear-shaped body in the reflection. *My arms look pretty good*, he thought. *Well, at least they do when I flex them.* He took a deep breath and tried to suck in his stomach. He was sensitive about the jiggle of his belly when it was touched. *See, I'm not fat. Right, LeBron? I know you agree, and I don't have to spend a million dollars a year on my body like you do.*

Realizing that he couldn't suck in his belly and breathe at the same time, he exhaled hard. He watched his body go from LeBron James back to Nigel Barnes.

"NIIII-GEL!" his mother called from the kitchen. Whenever she called his name, it sounded as if she were singing it. "Come for lunch!"

Nigel rushed to put his shirt back on. He darted down the stairs to see his father, his younger brother,

Jason, and his two teenage cousins Jalen and Leroy already sitting at the table, eating.

"Pudge, Pudge, where are you, Pudge? Fudge, Pudge, we see you, Pudgy," sang Leroy.

Nigel sighed, shook his head and took his seat between Jalen and Leroy. Nigel felt a tug at the back of his shirt as Jalen pulled at the white tag hanging off the back of his collar. In his hurry, Nigel had put his shirt on inside out.

"Dag, Pudge," said Jalen. "You was so hungry you couldn't even put your shirt on right? Whachu doin' up there, Sir Pudges, big belly dancing?"

Everyone at the table began laughing. Everyone except Nigel. Jalen and Leroy took turns poking Nigel's belly, giggling as if it were the funniest thing in the world. Nigel swatted at their hands like they were pesky flies.

"Stop it. Leave me, nuh. Stop!" cried Nigel.

"That's enough, leave Pudge alone," Nigel's father said, taking a sip of coffee. "Y'know, Nigel, I haven't received an email from Coach Shabaka yet saying he drafted you to his team. I hope you get him again this season. I like him."

"Yes, yes," Nigel's mother chimed in from the kitchen. "Nice man and I love his daughter. Pudge, you need to lose a little more weight to make that girl like you. She's so pretty, she probably has so many boys after her. You need to at least give yourself a chance and shed some pounds."

"Ya, fatty, you can't get the girl looking like that," said Jalen, snickering.

"Leave the boy alone," said Nigel's father. "He's not thinking about girls, yet. He plays ball. But to be a better baller, Nigel, you need to shed some pounds. Coach Shabaka and I spoke about that the other day."

"But Coach said I wasn't too fat to play. He said I was fine. He, he said I was like, ummm . . . Charles Zion?" Nigel claimed, close to tears.

"You mean Zion Williamson and Charles Barkley. Listen, both those players were effective on the court, but their playing weight was too heavy. Coach Shabaka was just too nice to say it in front of you, but everyone can see it. You need to drop some weight to be a better player! There's no such thing as a fat champion!"

Nigel's mood went from bad to worse at the notion of Coach Shabaka thinking he was overweight. He sat with his head down, staring woefully at how his belly folded over the waist of his pants. He tuned out his family's fat talk, wishing he was somewhere else.

★★★

The next week, Nigel received word that he was to join Coach Shabaka and the Power for another season. Nigel was the first player to enter the gym doors for the first practice, and he looked at the team list posted on the wall.

"Nigel! What's good, young blood?" Coach Shabaka said, giving Nigel a pound. "Glad to see you're here early, as usual. Well, you know what to do. Let's get down to business."

Nigel began to practise jumpshots as the other players trickled into the gym. He was excited to greet some of his old teammates and catch up. All the boys had entered the gym except for one. Nigel looked around at the boys on his team, feeling confident that he could lead them to a championship. *Even Asim and Sundeep are a lot better. We gonna get it this year*, Nigel thought as he watched his teammates shooting around.

Nigel noticed a couple guys who were new to the team. Amen Rauf, a six-foot-five thirteen-year-old, was incredibly strong looking. He resembled a football player more than a basketball player. *I need to get on his good side*, Nigel thought. Then there was a sharp shooter like Stephen Curry named Mohammad Waheed. Nigel knew he could rack up a gang of assists passing the ball to him. He made up the starting five in his head as he watched the rest of the boys hoist up shots. *Me and Omari should be a good backcourt. Not many teams can compete with us, we should go far.*

Just as Nigel thought that, the last player came into the gym with what looked like his whole family. Denham Dubois rushed in with his sneakers, tied together by the laces, hanging off his neck.

Nigel watched in shock as Denham sat on the bench and changed his shoes. *No way! That's Number 5 from summer league. He's on our team now? How could this happen?*

5 New TEAMMATE

Coach Shabaka walked through the gym, high-fiving and giving pounds to each player. When he saw Denham, his face broke into a wide grin. Nigel watched as Coach Shabaka greeted Denham's mother and siblings, then slapped hands with Denham like they were old friends — two open hand slaps, a back slap, a front clasp and a hug.

Coach don't greet me like that, Nigel thought, mean mugging Denham.

"Sup, Coach," Nigel heard Denham say. "Glad to be here. We going to do something special this year. I promise."

"That's what I like to hear! Denham, welcome to the squad. We're glad to have you!" Coach Shabaka yelled.

Most of the boys stopped shooting and focused on Coach Shabaka and the new player. Coach Shabaka blew the whistle and motioned for everyone to meet at centre court. The assistant coach, Coach Rodney, gathered the players trying to take last-second shots so that Coach Shabaka had the team's full attention.

"Okay, boys, look around," Coach Shabaka said. "This is our squad! This is our family. This is our championship team! We just have to go out there and prove it. Are y'all ready?"

The boys looked around the gym at each other, nodding.

"We ready, Coach!" a few of the boys replied in unison.

Coach Shabaka walked around the boys. "We have a few different players from last season, but the philosophy is still the same. Play lockdown defence and score easy. That's what we do. If you don't play defence, you don't play. Period. Okay, boys, let's get started. Coach Rodney, please get them warmed up."

Coach Rodney blew his whistle and told the boys to run a few laps around the court single file. Then he ran some light drills with the team and had them stretching in a circle around him at centre court.

After checking his cellphone for the itinerary, Coach Shabaka joined them. "This is what we do every practice. You come in here first thing before you start chasing each other around, hoisting up three-pointers and half-court shots. I want you to go as close to the basket as you can and make three of the easiest shots possible. Then move back a little and make some mid-range shots, then shoot your long-distance shots. All right?"

The boys all nodded. The new ones looked confused.

"Can anyone tell me why I want you to take easy

shots before trying to make difficult ones?" Coach Shabaka said.

Kash smiled and spoke before any of the other boys could raise their hands or respond. "It's because the more easy shots you make, the easier it makes the hard shots."

Coach Shabaka nodded in agreement while pointing at Kash with the index fingers of both hands. Right hand in front, left hand behind, switching them back and forth in rhythm as if it were a dance move.

"Oooowwweeee!!! I love that answer. Say it again, Kash!" Coach Shabaka demanded.

Kash repeated the reply while Coach Shabaka did his finger-pointing boogie. The boys all giggled as they watched Coach bouncing as if reggae music was playing.

"All right. All right, settle down," said Coach Shabaka "Let's get back to business. So after shoot-around, we'll run some drills. Then we stretch to complete our warm-up. Okay? Each practice I want one of you to lead the team in stretches. We'll switch to a new person each week. Any volunteers for next week?"

"I got that, Coach," Nigel said, quickly throwing up his hand.

"Excellent. Thank you, Nigel. Now, before we start practice, I think we should introduce ourselves. I once heard a wise man say that when teammates know each other's names, they tend to play better together, so we're going to get to know each other a little bit. We'll go in a circle. Tell us your name and what you want to improve in most in basketball this season. So I'll start. I think most of you know, I'm Coach Shabaka. This year I want to get better at helping players such as yourselves to achieve your goals. To my right, this guy here, with the whistle hanging from his neck, is Coach Rodney."

Coach Rodney introduced himself and what he wanted to get better at. "I want to improve my communication skills so I can one day become a head coach," he said.

Next to him was Omari, who said he wanted to become a better three-point shooter. Nigel said he wanted to improve his defence. Amritpal said he wanted to improve his dribbling. As the introductions went around, most of the boys began repeating what the others had already said, until they reached the last one in line.

He held his chin, looking at the ceiling as if the answer would fall onto his head. "My name is Denham and . . . And I want to learn to become a better leader. Both on and off the court."

Coach Shabaka said to Coach Rodney, "I knew there was something I liked about this boy. That's an excellent answer, son," he said to Denham. "I've never heard that answer before. You are going to achieve great things . . ."

Nigel leaned over to Omari and whispered, "Look at this guy. Trying to suck up already, on the first day."

Omari whispered back, "I know, right? Like, dude, c'mon now."

The boys snickered as Coach Shabaka continued. "All of you are destined for greatness. Not just in basketball. Each of you has something special to contribute to society, and one day soon you'll know exactly what it is. However, right now, what we're going to do is run some sprints. I want to see what kind of shape you're in. On this team we run, and we run a lot. We outrun every other team. So line up on the black baseline against the wall and, on my whistle, sprint as fast as you can to the other wall and back. Ten times! Everybody up!"

The boys all groaned as they rose to their feet.

"Do I need to make it twenty times? Hurry up, let's go!"

The boys rushed to the baseline to await the signal. Nigel sized up the competition. He loved to win races when other kids underestimated his speed due to his weight.

TWEEEEET. The boys dashed off the line like a team of race horses trying to earn top prize.

6 Exhibition GAME

"All right, team, this week's practice we're scrimmaging against the Bearcats," Coach Shabaka said to the boys as they sat on the gym floor. Nigel was familiar with Coach Shabaka's good friend Coach Jaden of the Bearcats from past exhibition games. The Bearcats played in the Mississauga league, about a twenty-minute drive away from Brampton, so the Power and the Bearcats frequently sharpened skills against each other.

The two coaches stood mid-court, chatting while their teams did a shoot-around. The teams mirrored each other, as boys on both teams took close shots then backed up a little further as they made each basket. Nigel thought, *Coach Shabaka and Coach Jaden really share the same philosophy. The Bearcats are just like us. They gonna be tough.*

Nigel started shooting on the main basket with a few of the regulars from the Power — Omari, Kash and Asim. They worked together, rebounding the ball and getting it out to the next shooter. Nigel chased a rebound that went toward where Denham was dribbling. The boys stood face to face and gave each other a challenging look. Denham was the first to break the glare. In a playful manner, he elbow-jabbed Nigel in the ribs.

"Oh, wow, look at that jiggle. Yo, did anyone ever tell you that you could be a belly dancer?" laughed Denham. Nigel bit his lip and breathed heavily as Denham continued. "So, fat boy, looks like we're teammates, bruh. I ain't tripping about before. That's all water off a duck now. Know what I'm saying? You're pretty good. But I'm better and I'm gonna take over your team. Just know that."

Nigel held back the urge to body check the smug smile right off Denham's face.

"Jus' playing, yo. Don't be so serious," Denham said, chuckling.

"We'll see," Nigel replied and dribbled back to the main basket.

This guy ain't gonna see one pass from me this season, Nigel thought. *Matter of fact, I'm gonna freeze his whole game. Ain't no one gonna pass to him.*

"Hey, guys, come here," Nigel said to Omari, Kash and Asim. He motioned with his hand for the four of them to huddle together.

"What's up, Nige?" asked Asim.

"Yo, guys. You know we're good enough to win the championship this season, right?"

"Of course we are. We getting it done this season," said Kash.

"Okay, so we have to stick together. We're the core of this team. I've played with you guys for, like, four seasons, right? Two summer leagues and two winters. So we family. We can't let just anyone come in here and mess up our flow —"

"What are you getting at, Nige?" Omari cut in. "We boys, we fam. Nothing breaks us up. No one gets in our way."

"Exactly!" Nigel replied. "That's what I'm saying. We don't need outsiders. That guy Denham is an outsider. He don't belong here."

The boys all looked at each other, shocked by what Nigel was saying. They all peered at Denham out of the corners of their eyes.

Kash leaned in closer and lowered his voice to a whisper. "My dude, what are you saying? Denham seems cool. And he can ball."

"He's not one of us!" Nigel quickly responded. "Don't you guys remember in the summer? He played for the Tigers. He wore number five. They made fun of us. Called us names and fouled us on purpose when the ref wasn't looking."

"Ya, we almost had a brawl against those fools," said Omari.

Nigel motioned for the boys to huddle even closer and whispered, "Look we don't need Number 5 on our team to win. Don't need him. Don't want him."

"Okay, but what can we do about that?" asked Asim. "Coach chose him for our team."

"I've got a plan. Listen close. Something that will send him home crying to his mama," said Nigel.

They were interrupted by a ball bouncing into the huddle. Sundeep ran over to retrieve it. "What's up, fellas! We having a meeting?"

"Hey, Sun," the boys replied separately. Nigel waved Sundeep off as if nothing interesting was going on. "No meeting. Just telling jokes," he said.

Sundeep's expression showed confusion. "Jokes? But no one's laughing. Sure you're not having a meeting?"

Nigel tried to keep the annoyance out of his voice. "Nah, bredrin, no meeting. I'm just not that funny. That's all. I need better jokes."

The other boys began to laugh at Nigel.

"Oh, look. Now these guys are laughing. I guess I'm getting funnier already."

"Whatever, Nigel," said Sundeep. "You act weird sometimes." He dribbled back to the basket he had come from.

"Yo, why you ain't tell Sundeep the plan?" asked Kash. "He been around from the beginning like the rest of us. He's core squad."

"True," said Nigel. "But I don't know if he can be trusted. He and Denham go to the same school. Not that they are friends or anything. But look, they already talking to each other. Sun might feel guilty, tell him and spoil everything."

The boys all nodded in agreement, then huddled close to listen to Nigel's plan.

A few minutes later, Coach Shabaka and Coach Jaden blew their whistles to begin practice. As usual, the boys ran drills, sprints and more drills. They discussed game situations and defensive principles.

"Remember, stay low on defence. Hands up at all times. Move your feet — don't reach. If you reach, the ref will call a foul. Just stay in front of your man. If everyone does that, we'll force turnovers and get fast-break opportunities," said Coach Shabaka. The boys all nodded. "All right. You boys ready to scrimmage?"

"Yah!!!" the boys yelled and started pounding balls on the floor with excitement.

"Okay. Settle down, boys. Put your balls on the side and we'll get started. Hurry up, I got something for you."

Coach Rodney was carrying two giant, see-through bags of uniforms. When the boys noticed, they crowded around him, jumping up and down. Coach Rodney neatly spread a few of the jerseys on the gym floor. The boys were hypnotized by the stunning black jerseys with bold, bright-green letters that read POWER. The jerseys also had a shiny red patch under the collar that read POWER.

"Coach, you changed our colours! We're not powder blue anymore?" said Sundeep.

"That's correct. I had the chance to upgrade our uniforms. The colours are important to me, as they represent the African Liberation flag created with the support of Marcus Mosiah Garvey. Most of you might remember me talking about him during summer league."

"Ya, I remember you telling us about Marcus Garvey," said Nigel. "That he was a journalist and poet. And that he tried to unite Black people around the world."

"That's correct. He wanted Black people to be proud of themselves, despite the negative things others would say about them. He wanted people to know their history, and said that a people without knowledge of their past is like . . ."

Some of the boys joined in, ". . . like a tree without roots."

"Exactly. Yes, you boys do remember. The colours represent African liberation and unity around the world. Red is for the blood that unites all people. Black represents people of African ancestry. And green is for the land and abundant natural wealth of Africa. They are a symbol of African people, here in North America and around the world. These colours say we share the same history and will share the same destiny of freedom as well."

"So . . . when we wear these colours it means we are freedom fighters?" Amen said jokingly. The boys laughed.

Coach Shabaka chuckled and replied, "You know what? Yes. Yes, you are. But not only when you wear these uniforms. Every day. Everywhere you go, you should represent freedom and unity for all people. No matter what they look like. We should accept people for who they are."

The boys sat quietly, nodding their heads, until Coach Shabaka shouted, "Now who wants to wear number thirty-two? How about number eleven . . . and number twenty-three?"

7 Kiss, Spin, SWISH

You would think it was Christmas morning, the way each boy was grinning ear to ear. Coach Rodney distributed uniforms to each eager player like a basketball Santa Claus.

"And, boys," he said, "don't forget to take a pair of shorts in the same size as your jersey. All right, I got two jerseys left. Number thirteen and number five. Who wants it?"

The last two players without jerseys were Omari and Denham. They threw their hands up at the same time and yelled, "I'll take number five!"

Nigel and Omari looked at each other. Omari's jersey number for the last four seasons had been number five. Nigel knew that he liked wearing it because his birthday was March 5. Nigel remembered Omari's birthday parties when they were kids — every year he wore a new sports jersey with the number five on it. Football, soccer, basketball — even hockey — number five jerseys in an array of colours hung in his closet.

"Omari has been number five from the first day he played for the Power. We should honour that, don't you think?" Nigel said to the coaches.

Denham jumped up to counter Nigel's argument. "I've always worn number five. It's my favourite number. I've never worn anything else since I started playing ball."

Coach Rodney looked over at Coach Shabaka and shrugged his shoulders. Coach Shabaka smiled and said, "Looks like we have a shootout."

The boys in the gym all began to howl, "Ooooouuuuu! Shootout! Showdown!"

"Omari, Denham, you guys are gonna have to shoot for it," said Coach Shabaka. "Free throws. Omari, you go first. You guys will shoot until one of you misses and the other one makes."

Nigel instructed Omari as he stepped up to the free-throw line. "Come on, bruh, you got this. I know you're nervous. Just do it like we practised. That's your number. We ain't gonna let that clown beat us," Nigel said.

Omari had never been a great free-throw shooter. Nigel had told him to always be repetitive when taking free throws, because it would help calm the nerves and focus on making the shot. So that's what Omari did. One dribble on his right side, one dribble on his left. Omari bent his knees, made sure his shooting elbow stayed close to his body and released the ball with backspin.

SWISH.

Kiss, Spin, Swish

Omari walked away from the line victorious. Nigel threw up his fist in celebration. They were quickly brought down to earth. Denham coolly walked to the line, blew a kiss at the basket, spun the ball on his palm and drained the shot with ease.

The boys in the gym cheered as Omari and Denham made four shots each.

On the fifth shot, Nigel jumped to his feet, sensing that Omari was getting nervous again. He threw his arm around Omari's shoulder and whispered, "Yo, I know you want to win that number bad. Trust the routine. You almost missed that last shot cuz you didn't do your two dribbles first. Do it the exact same every time, all right?"

Omari nodded and went through his routine. But Nigel knew Omari's concentration was off. As the ball left Omari's hand, Nigel knew right away it was off too. He felt bad for his friend as he watched the ball clank off the front of the rim and dive to the floor. A dejected Omari walked off the line and plunked down beside Nigel.

They watched Denham take his fifth shot the same way he took the previous four. Same routine, same result. *Kiss, spin, SWISH.* Denham had won the shootout. The number five jersey was his. The boys cheered and clapped hands for Denham.

Instead of celebrating his win, Denham walked directly over to Omari to dap fists with him. "Good shooting, yo. I got lucky, don't sweat it. You're a nice player, bruh."

Omari sluggishly raised his fist and dapped Denham without saying a word. Coach Rodney walked over to Omari with the jerseys and patted him on his shoulder to try to comfort him as Omari reluctantly took the number thirteen.

Nigel watched Coach Rodney hand jersey number five to Denham. He wanted to wipe the smug smile off of Denham's face. Coach Rodney shook hands with both boys to let them know how proud he was of them for the poise they showed. "It's not easy to shoot when everything's quiet and everyone is watching you. You guys did good. You'll be stronger for this, trust me. Omari don't hang your head. You both will have a special year this season. I guarantee. Now, the rest of you. Ready for that scrimmage?"

The boys howled with excitement as Coach Shabaka headed toward mid-court. He waved at Coach Jaden to let him know that he was ready to scrimmage. Coach Jaden raised his chin and held up his index finger mouthing the words, "One minute."

The coaches returned attention back to their teams to announce starting lineups. "Okay, boys, this is our first game together. Just go out there and have fun. I know Coach Jaden's style. His boys will be intense, just like us. Okay. Hands in."

The boys all threw their hands to the middle.

"Oh, ya, we going to do the cheer a little different. Instead of one-two-three, Power, I'm going to say something else. And at the end, you guys yell 'Power.' Okay?"

The boys looked around at each other, excited, as Coach belted out, "I . . . have the . . ."

Right on cue the boys screamed, "POWER!!!" and jumped around like a pack of berserk animals.

As the game progressed, Nigel's plan worked masterfully. He and the core group did not pass the ball to Denham, even when he was wide open under the basket. They took the shot themselves or passed it to someone else. They had shared the plan with the rest of the team, with the exception of the new guys and Sundeep. Chance after chance, Denham would be denied. He faked a cut to the three-point line, went back door with his hand high. But Nigel pretended he didn't see Denham and took the shot himself. No one else seemed to notice, because the shot went in.

Denham tried setting a pick for Asim, then popped out to the three-point line. The correct play would be to throw the ball out to Denham. Instead, Asim spun out of the double team and found himself an open layup. Again no one noticed the plan in action. However, Nigel was beginning to suspect that Denham knew something from his look of frustration after not getting the ball. *It's working*, Nigel laughed to himself.

At the half, Denham approached the boys about it.

"Hey, y'all, these guys are leaving me open all over the court. Find me. Those are easy scores."

Asim, Kash and Nigel looked at each other in shock, as if they didn't know what was going on.

"Oh, my bad, my fault," Nigel said. "We'll keep an eye out for that next time."

They all went back out to play the second half. The same thing kept happening, so Denham found other ways to contribute. He grabbed offensive rebounds. He played the passing lanes and got steals. Anything he could do to help the team win, he did it. Despite the boys not passing to him, Denham still finished with fifteen points, fifteen rebounds, five steals and five assists.

After the game, Coach Shabaka let them know how impressed he was with their play, especially on defence. "Good win, boys. Now I have bragging rights over Coach Jaden, so thank you. Big up our leading scorer Nigel with twenty-one points. All of you. Good job. Just one thing. You have to remain aware on offence. Keep your head up and look for the open man. A number of times we had guys open to score but you didn't notice. So just be aware. Okay? And make sure you wash your jerseys. Don't roll up to the gym with a cloud of five-day funk following your uniform."

Nigel was smiling to himself. Not for the win — he was proud of the success of his plan to wound Denham.

8 Game ONE

As Nigel walked in with his father, the gym was lively with the sound of sneakers screeching on the floor. Referee whistles chirped, basketballs pounded and the applause from the bleachers was loud as families cheered for their boys. All four basketball courts had league games going.

Coach Shabaka and Nigel's father shook hands, while Nigel tossed his gym bag to the floor and began to dribble the ball between his legs. Denham, his mother, his brothers and his sister were next to appear. Coach Shabaka waved his hand high so they could see him through all the commotion in the gym.

"Hey, Coach," Denham said, dapping Coach Shabaka's fist.

"Hey, Denham. Good to see you guys. Why don't you warm up with Nigel? Do some chest passes." Denham dropped his bag, ball and water bottle against the wall then stood at a distance, facing Nigel. The boys nodded at each other as Coach Shabaka turned his attention to Denham's mother.

These are the only passes he gonna see from me today, Nigel thought. He put a little extra push on his chest pass, making Denham stumble backward a little when he caught it.

"I hope it's not a problem that I can't stay today," Denham's mother said. "I have some errands."

"Oh, that's no issue at all," said Coach Shabaka. "Do what you need to do. He's in good hands."

Strange, all the other kids' parents stay during their games, Nigel thought. Some even brought other relatives and friends to watch their kids play. This was the first time he had seen a kid not have someone in the stands cheering for them. *His parents probably don't like him either,* Nigel thought as he caught the pass back from Denham.

Denham's mother bent down to give him a hug and kiss. "Now you make sure you don't give Coach any trouble, all right? I'll see you later. Have a great game, honey!"

Nigel hurled a hard pass toward Denham as he was waving at his mother and not fully paying attention. The speeding ball grazed Denham's shoulder and nearly hit him in the head. "Whoa! That was a close one," Denham said, laughing as he ran to retrieve the ball.

Not close enough, Nigel thought.

Before long, all of the Power players were warming up around the coach — dribbling, passing balls, some just chit-chatting. They looked like a red, black and green army in their uniforms.

Once their court was free, Coach Shabaka gathered the boys together. "We're on court number four, boys. Follow me."

He led the boys through the waiting area like Moses parting the Red Sea as other coaches and players were still waiting for their court to be free.

"All right, boys," he said. "Take the far bench, drop your belongings there and begin our warm-up routine on the opposite basket. Let's go!"

The boys ran to the bench and began their warm-up, jogging in single file behind Nigel. They ran three laps around the half court, then split into two lines at the three-point line to run the layup drill. One line had balls to take shots while the other line rebounded and passed the ball back to the next player in line.

"C'mon, faster, let's go! Game speed," hollered Coach Rodney. Coach Shabaka was at the scoring table passing on the lineups to the high-school student volunteer scorekeepers. The opposing team entered a little later and began their warm-ups on the other basket. The Gryphons' uniforms were royal blue with white lettering, white numbers and a white picture of a gryphon — body of a lion, and head and wings of an eagle — on the chest.

After the buzzer, the boys huddled around the coaches on the bench, sipping on their water bottles.

They were all excited, hoping to hear their names in the starting lineup.

"Boys, this is the real deal," said Coach Shabaka. "It's not practice anymore. This game counts, so let's do it the way we practised. I want to see strong defence. Stay low, move your feet quickly and stay in front of your man. Keep your arms up so you can deflect any passes they make. On offence, let's move the ball around. Let everyone get a touch. Be assertive, drive the ball to hole and find the open man if you don't have an easy shot. Okay. Starting the game will be Kash, Nigel, Asim, Amen and . . ."

Nigel knew Omari was hoping to hear his name next, but he knew what was about to happen. Omari had started for the Power ever since he joined the squad, but Nigel had a feeling that was about to end today. He was right.

". . . and we'll have Denham join those four as the fifth starter," finished Coach Shabaka.

Nigel gave Omari a look that said, *Don't worry, we going to handle him for you.* He wasn't going to let Denham steal Omari's spot.

"You got that, boys! Let's go out there and win one. Hands in. Who got the Power?!"

The boys were so hyped they were springing on their toes. They crammed their hands to the middle then screamed, "I've got the POWER!" Jumping up and down, the starters headed to centre court for the jump ball while everyone else bounced to the bench.

The referees took their spots on the court, one on the sideline and the other holding the ball at mid-court for the jump. The boys all froze in place, waiting for the referee's signal. Amen was taking the jump for the Power.

TWEET! The referee blew the whistle and lobbed the ball above the boys' heads to start the game. Amen leaped as high as he could, just outstretching the reach of the Gryphons centre to win the tip and tap the ball back into the hands of Denham. When Nigel saw the ball go toward Denham, he ran over, clapping his hands, and said, "Okay, I got it from here. Give it to me. I'll set up the play."

Denham waved him off saying, "No worries, bruh, I got it."

Nigel wasn't about to let Denham take over his position too. Reluctantly, he took his stance on the left wing near the three-point line as Denham guided the offence from the top of the key. Amen darted to the top of the key to set a pick on Denham's man. Denham crossed his man over, right into the chest of Amen, and dribbled toward the basket as Amen's defender tried to cut off Denham's path to the basket. Seeing this, Amen quickly rolled toward the rim, creating a two-on-one, just like the drills they did in training. Denham spied Amen coming opposite the defender and tossed a one-handed bounce pass between the defender's legs to Amen, who caught the ball in stride for an open layup. The boys on the bench for the Power all jumped up, clapping their hands, excited that they were the first to score.

9 Teamwork, OR LACK OF IT

Coach Rodney nodded at Coach Shabaka. "The two new guys worked that pick and roll to perfection. Good teamwork. Not a bad pick-up, Coach."

Everyone on the Power seemed happy about the score, except for Nigel. He was still upset about not getting to handle the ball for the first play. *I could've done that*, he thought.

The Power players got back on defence quickly. They played their men close and forced the Gryphons to put up a difficult shot, which Amen rebounded and tossed ahead to Denham, who was breaking to the basket. Two defenders for the Gryphons were already back, so Denham had to pull the ball out and wait for the rest of his team to come up the court. Once everyone was in place, Denham passed the ball to Nigel, who was standing at the top of the three-point line. Denham's man wasn't paying attention. So he flashed down the lane, wide open, hands up high, so that Nigel could see him and drop an easy assist for the score. Instead, Nigel hurled a pass to the opposite side where Kash was standing. Kash's defender was stuck between covering him and Denham, so he left Kash open in case Kash passed it to Denham for the easier score. If the other team knew about the plan, they could've left Denham open the whole game. Kash threw up a long-range shot that rattled off the rim.

Coach Shabaka jumped to his feet. "C'mon, boys, pass to the open man! We just lost two points there. C'mon, now!"

The Power boys made the game difficult for themselves by not sharing the ball with Denham. Despite the self-sabotage, the game was still close by the end of the third quarter. The intensity was high, and the game was beginning to get chippy. The teams were arguing, bumping into opposing players after the whistle was blown.

When the game resumed, Kash was dribbling to the rim, thinking he had an open lane to finish with a basket. The defender had baited him, knowing exactly where he was going with the ball. The defender stepped in front of Kash as he leaped off the ground. Instead of flying high, Kash was quickly grounded. The referee blew the whistle again.

"Chaaarge!" he yelled, while making the offensive foul signal. Kash and the defender from the Gryphons, Number 11, were lying side by side on the floor, watching the referee. Number 11 gave a fist pump when he heard the call. His teammates rushed to help him off the ground. Kash, meanwhile, stayed on his back with his hands covering his face.

"Don't cry, baby," Number 11 said to Kash as he jumped to his feet.

Kash looked up as three players from the Gryphons stood over him.

"Don't cry! Poor baby, don't cry. Ou ou ou," they wailed, rubbing their eyes like an infant trying to hold back tears. They crowded around Kash, keeping him from rising to his feet. Right away, Denham ran over and started pushing the Gryphon players away from Kash.

"Get off him! Get out of here!" Denham hollered. He stood nose to nose with the Gryphons with his fists clenched, ready to stand up for Kash even if it meant a fight. The Gryphon players were surprised, and a little scared of Denham's aggression. They ran back to their bench making sobbing noises, "boo woo woo," still trying to tease Kash.

Denham held out his hand to help Kash off the ground. *I hope Kash spits at Denham's hand*, Nigel thought. Kash hesitated, but no other teammates had come to back him up. Not even Nigel, who was watching from a distance.

"Thanks, bruh," Kash said as they gripped hands.

Denham hoisted him to his feet. "No worries, yo. Those boys are soft. They can't mess with us. We the Power!" said Denham with passion.

Kash looked at him in shock. Then slowly nodded his head, saying, "Ya. Ya, you know that's right. We the Power, bruh!"

They pounded fists and ran back to the bench.

The Power were down by one. If they could force the Gryphons to miss, they would have the last shot and a chance to win the game. Coach Shabaka subbed in Omari, because he was the best defender on the team. On the floor to finish the game were Kash, Nigel, Omari, Amen and Denham — good defenders that would give them a chance to stop the Gryphons.

Number 11 for the Gryphons caught the inbound pass on his side of the court and dribbled slowly to the half line, trying to kill time. There were only twenty seconds left on the clock. Coach Shabaka had instructed the boys to stay in the half court and pretend they weren't ready to play defence until Number 11 dribbled over the half line. As soon as he did, Omari and Denham pounced at the ball, trapping Number 11 in the corner — the half-court trap. Number 11 panicked and tried to dribble out of trouble, but Denham was able to poke the ball away, right into the hands of Omari. Denham took off, sprinting to the basket, looking for the pass, while being chased by Gryphon players. None were in front of him. It would've been an easy two points to win the game if Omari pitched the ball up ahead. Instead, he kept it, dribbling to the basket as fast as he could move. With the clock winding down, players and spectators in the gym were screaming the countdown, "Four-three-two-one!"

Omari lobbed the ball forward from the three-point line as the buzzer sounded. *SWISH!* The ball dropped through the net, not touching any part of the rim. Omari jumped up and punched the air with elation. A three-pointer to win the game.

Nigel was the first to leap on Omari, excited because he didn't pass the ball to Denham, and kept it from being Denham celebrating the game-winning shot. Nigel was so proud that they had stolen that moment from Denham, the same way Denham had stolen Omari's number and starting position on the team. The boys were so busy celebrating, they didn't notice Coach Shabaka arguing with the referee, who was waving his hands, saying, "No good. The basket's no good. It was too late."

"Are you sure? It looked like it left his hand on time," pleaded Coach Shabaka.

"Sorry. He was still holding the ball when the clock hit zero. Sorry. Very sorry. Gryphons win."

10 I'M OUT

Nigel and the Power players watched the Gryphons screaming in celebration. Covering his face with both hands, Nigel went from extreme happiness to heart-breaking sorrow in seconds.

Both coaches gathered their boys for the post-game handshake. The Power boys could barely keep their heads up as they slapped hands with the energized Gryphon players. Once through the line, the Gryphon players roared with glee and ran back to their bench.

"So, boys, tell me," said Coach Shabaka. "Why all the fighting today? What's going on with y'all? Are we not able to play competitively without having to throw hands?"

The boys looked around at each other. None of them wanted to answer.

"Well, don't talk all at once, now," said Coach Shabaka.

Kash spoke up first. "Those guys kept calling us sissies and WNBA."

"Ya, they was saying we play like girls and that only girls cry for fouls," said Nigel.

"Plus they were cussing at us," Asim said. "Calling us wimps and weak."

"They said we were mama's boys —" Tony began, but was cut off by Coach Shabaka.

"Okay, I get it. Stop right there. First, I'm a mama's boy. I love my mama and always will. Do you think I'm soft?"

The boys shook their heads.

"Am I correct in saying that all of you have mothers?"

The boys all nodded in agreement.

"And do your mothers take care of you and love you?"

Again the boys nodded.

"So it's not a disrespectful thing if someone says that to you. You thank them and walk away, because you know the truth — that you have a mother who loves and cares for you. Perhaps they don't have a mother who cares, which is why they're trying to make you feel bad. But you guys should never feel bad for that. I've met all your mothers and they are beautiful people!"

The boys shuffled their feet uncomfortably as Coach Shabaka continued. "Second! If they're calling you WNBA, keep in mind, the WNBA is a professional basketball league. WNBA players get paid to play because they are some the best athletes in the world. You boys should feel honoured to even get close to what those women have achieved with this game. So I don't want to hear again that you feel disrespected for foolish things other kids say to you."

After Coach Shabaka's talk, Nigel and Kash quickly packed up their things from the bench and headed to the change room. Nigel leaned close to Kash as they walked, saying, "Don't sweat it, yo. We'll do better next week. Could've swore we were gonna win today."

"Ya, whatevs," Kash replied.

"Hey, good thinking out there. Letting Denham pick you up. Make him believe you're his friend so he won't suspect anything," Nigel said.

Kash gave Nigel an icy glare. "Don't congratulate me for that. It's because of your stupid plan we lost the game today. If Omari would've passed the ball to Denham, we'd be the ones celebrating now."

"Hey, man. We still came close. It's the referee's fault—"

"Don't give me that. It ain't about the referee. We lost the game because we ain't playing right. We work so hard, for what? To shoot ourselves in the foot! Nah, man. I'm not with this."

"Oh, come on, Kash. Be cool. Once we get Denham to quit, we go back to normal. Everything will be cool. Trust me."

"Trust you? How can I trust you? Look what happened when those guys weren't letting me get up. Where were you, huh? Where were any of you! Denham was the only one who had my back. He was ready to throw down, while you guys just watched."

"Nah, it's not like that, bruh. Can't say that. We boys. Look how many times I had your back before."

"True, but this time you didn't. I'm out, man. I ain't doing your plan no more. You guys can keep going. I won't say nothing to Coach, but I ain't doing it no more."

Kash left Nigel in the change room. Deep down, Nigel knew what Kash was saying was true. But he had convinced himself that his plan was necessary.

Nigel returned to the gym as Coach Shabaka was ushering the remaining boys to the sidelines where their parents were waiting. All except Denham, who was looking around for his. Nigel smirked as Denham dropped his bag to the floor in disappointment.

Coach Shabaka said, "Don't worry, son. You can hang out with me and Nigel until your mother gets here. Nigel's father said he'd be a little late too, so we can wait for your mother here until she comes."

Denham shook his head. "No. No. My dad's supposed to get me today. I'm going to his place for the rest of the weekend."

Suddenly, Denham scooped up his belongings. "Dad!" he yelled, as a tall man hurried over in their direction.

Coach Shabaka approached him with his hand extended. "Hi, there. I'm Coach —"

"Shabaka," Denham's father finished the

introduction. "Yes, I'm D's father, Grantley. Sorry I'm late. I hope I haven't kept you long."

"Oh, no. We just finished. No problem."

"Hey, Dad," said Denham. "I gotta go to the washroom. Watch my stuff, okay?"

"Ya go ahead D. You know where it is?"

Denham nodded and ran off.

Denham's father scooped up Denham's basketball and began spinning it on his middle finger. He nodded at Nigel, who was fascinated by the spinning trick. Nigel tried unsuccessfully to spin his ball on his finger too.

Coach Shabaka was also impressed. "So you play?"

"Used to. Not so much now. Old age, injuries and work get in the way. I got to live my basketball dreams through D now," Denham's dad laughed.

"I hear you, brother. It's not as easy as it used to be. Coaching is the only time I get on the court these days. Sometimes I barely have time for that."

"Well, you must be doing something right. D talks about you and the Power all the time. You got him running around the house yelling, 'I have the Power!' He really likes you, Coach. So thank you. During this time he needs this. His mother and I are going through a separation, and I know it's hard on him. I try to keep things as normal as possible. But it can never be normal enough, unless things go back to the way they were. And I don't think they ever will."

So . . . Denham's parents are separating, Nigel thought.

I'm Out

That's interesting. Bet he feels real bad about it too. They'll probably get a divorce, then he'll be stuck in a custody battle. Well, I don't feel sorry for him.

"Denham is a good kid," said his dad. "He has trouble making new friends. And keeping them. He's been in a few fights at school, and I know it's because of me and his mother. He suppresses the anger, acts shy. But like a volcano, he can erupt. So if you can look out for him, maybe help him get comfortable with everyone, that will be really good for him."

"Ya, no doubt, no problem. I've seen him talking basketball and joking with a couple of the boys, so he's already off to a good start."

Nigel couldn't believe what he was hearing. *He's a good kid, what? Menace is more like it. That guy ain't shy. He's a tyrant. He may have the grown-ups fooled, but I'll expose him for who he really is.*

Coach Shabaka and Denham's dad dapped fists as Denham scurried back to where the men were standing.

"Let's go, Dad," Denham said. "Remember, you said you would play the new NBA 2K game with me tonight."

"All right, lil man. Say bye to Coach."

"Bye, Coach!" Denham said excitedly. Then he turned to Nigel and said, "Later, guy."

"Ya, later," Nigel replied.

Nigel watched Denham leave with his father, thinking of a way that he could use the news of the separation against his rival.

11 | I Know What's GOING ON HERE

Kiya was practising her jumpshots while the coaches prepared the gym. The players who had played on the Power in previous seasons knew who Kiya was and greeted her with high-fives. When Nigel saw her, he quickly headed in her direction.

"Hey, Key, sup? What you doing here? I didn't know you were coming." Nigel tried to conceal his excitement.

"Sup, Nige," Kiya replied, bumping Nigel playfully with her shoulder. "Thought I'd come and help you guys out a little. Heard you guys were struggling and could use a woman's touch."

"Ya, we lost last game. But I think we're gonna turn things around. What we need is for you to play for the team. I know at least one player I'd trade to have you play for us instead."

"Oh, you're so sweet, Nige. That's cute. Are you sure you'd want that? You would have to take a back seat to me as the star player on the team. I know how jealous you can get, hun." Kiya squeezed his cheek. She then dropped her ball, swiped Nigel's ball out of his hands and threw up a shot from half court. *THWIP.* The ball plunged right through the net.

The boys in the gym all turned around to see the deep shot Kiya made. "Oops, did I do that?" Kiya said, pretending to be bashful.

Nigel was hurrying to pick up his ball when he saw Denham rushing in with his mother, sister and brothers. Denham tossed his coat into the corner and quickly began to lace up his sneakers. Coach Shabaka said, "Nice to see you, D. Hurry, okay? We're about to get started."

Coach Rodney blew the whistle to notify the boys to stop shooting and join him at centre court. Most of the boys ran, dribbling their balls to the middle. Amritpal, Tony and Mohammad tried to make one more shot. The coaches glared at the three boys but said nothing. Tony turned to Coach Shabaka and said, "Hey, Coach. We gonna scrimmage today?"

Coach Shabaka replied, "Scrimmage? If we can't even begin practice on time, there'll be no time for scrimmage."

The other boys quickly began to plead with Amritpal, Tony and Mohammad to stop taking shots.

"Now, boys, I'm going to tell you this one time only," said Coach Shabaka. "When you hear the whistle, stop what you're doing and get to the middle.

And when Coach Rodney or I speak, we should not hear any bouncing —"

That moment, Tony's ball slipped out of his hand and it clapped against the hardwood floor.

"This is exactly what I'm talking about. Congratulations, you've won an all-expense-paid trip to the baseline," Coach Shabaka said in a game-show-host voice. "Let's go, gentlemen. Line up on the baseline. You won't need your balls. Leave them under the benches."

The boys complained under their breath as they followed Coach Shabaka's instructions.

"Are you making us run suicides? How many?" asked Amen.

"Yes and no. Yes we're going to run, but we don't call them suicides. Not on this team. We call them baselines. Running is good for you and it's fun, so we don't refer to them in a negative way. So that's what we're going to do. We're going to run baselines."

"Coach? Why do you keep saying we? Are you running with us?" Denham asked jokingly.

"That's a great question, D. As a matter of fact I am running with y'all. We're a team, so we do things together. But there's a catch. If I'm the first one to finish, you guys gotta run five extra baselines. So I hope you guys are ready, because I never lose a race. Okay, line it up, we're doing ten baselines. Sprint to half, touch the line with both hands, run backward back to this baseline, then sprint to the opposite baseline and run backward again back to this baseline. That equals one. All right. When Coach Rodney blows the whistle, off we go. Ready?"

TWEET! Coach Rodney blew the whistle and off they went. Omari and Denham were the fastest boys on the team, but they couldn't keep up with Coach Shabaka. Once the players completed their ten baselines, Coach Shabaka allowed them to catch their breath for forty-five seconds before doing the next five. This time Tony was the first to finish.

"Wasn't that fun, guys?" asked Coach Shabaka.

"Oh, ya, sure, whatever. Great fun," mumbled the boys sarcastically.

"I'm glad you guys enjoyed that, because we're going to do some more."

"What?!" the boys screamed.

"Yes, but not yet. First let's big up Tony for winning the baselines drill. Tony, you get the chance to choose our next drill. Defence, rebounding, shooting or layups?"

"Let's do defence first," said Tony.

"Excellent choice. Defence it will be. But first, I'd like to introduce someone to you. This lovely young lady who has been running with you today is my daughter, Kiya. Say hello, everyone."

"Hey, Kiya!" the boys yelled.

"All right, lady and gents. Go get some water and

meet me back here at centre court. We have a few things to discuss," said Coach Shabaka.

The players sprinted to grab their water bottles, then sat down at centre with the coaches.

"So last game was a tough one. We lost for a few reasons. First, you let that team's teasing get under your skin. We can't let that happen. You need to ignore the things the other team says to you. We know who we are. We are champions. Don't let anyone tell you otherwise. We are champions. Every time we step on this court, we do it as champions. No one else can tell you what you are when you know who you are. All the hard work you put into this game, the practise, the repetition, makes each and every one of you a champion. You understand me?"

The players nodded in agreement.

"Good. The second reason we lost the game was a lack of teamwork. Sometimes you guys look great out there. You swing the ball to the open man and get great-looking shots. Other times, you force up shots when you're already covered by two or three players. Even LeBron James and Stephen Curry don't do that. You can't do it all yourself. When there's a man open for an easier shot, that's the shot we want. You got to make that pass. A few times I could swear that y'all were not passing the ball to the open man on purpose. There were a couple of times I saw Denham wide open and some of you refused to pass it to him. What part of the game is that? That's not how I taught you to play. I know what's going on here . . ."

The players who were in on the plan gasped and looked nervously at each other. Nigel kept his head down the whole time.

". . . I figure that, because Denham is one of the new guys, you might not trust him to make the shot yet. Which really doesn't make sense, because he's one of the better shooters on the team. But maybe you just don't have the chemistry yet. So I understand."

Nigel took a deep breath, relieved that Coach Shabaka didn't know the real reason they weren't passing to Denham.

"So to help you out, I've come up with a few plays to keep every player involved in the game."

12 AMMUNITION

It was game day and the Power players were prepared to get their first win of the season. After the last practice, the boys didn't dare try to execute Plan No-Pass again. Coach Shabaka had had them run through his plays for what felt like a million times. They had it memorized — where they were supposed to stand, run and cut. They knew it so well, they could do it with their eyes closed. The Power players ran the plays in the game the same way they had in practice, and they scored easy baskets.

As usual, the players followed Nigel's example. Today, Nigel was forced to pass the ball to Denham. One of Coach Shabaka's plays required all the players to spread out on the court while Nigel dribbled the ball to the middle. This forced the man covering Denham to try to double team Nigel, leaving Denham wide open to receive the pass and score. No one else on the team would be open, so Nigel had no choice but to make the pass to Denham. If Nigel tried to take the shot himself over the double team, he knew Coach Shabaka would sit him on the bench.

After the other players saw Nigel make the pass, they began to pass to Denham as well. They passed the ball to him so often that Denham finished with thirty-six points, setting a record for the most points ever scored by a Power player. The Power won the game 85–43, a blowout win against the Warriors. Everyone on the Power scored at least one basket. After shaking hands with the other team, the Power players ran back to the bench screaming with excitement.

Nigel ground his teeth as he watched players give Denham high-fives and congratulate him on the great game. Nigel had held the highest scoring record before Denham broke it. Nigel knew he had to come up with another plan to get Denham off the team, or at least make Denham hurt.

As the other players were leaving to meet their families, Denham walked over to Nigel. "Yo, Nige."

"My name is Nigel."

"Oh, sorry. I thought . . . well, anyway, great game today, guy. You must've had at least ten assists to me alone. You probably finished with about eighteen to twenty assists. That's incredible! I couldn't have scored as many points without your passes. You were on point, yo."

Nigel nodded and looked away.

Denham continued, "Yo. I think you and I, we

make a really good team. There's no backcourt that's as fast and as skilled as us. We are going to tear this league apart!"

"Ya, whatevs," Nigel replied flatly.

Denham looked confused, but he held out his fist to dap Nigel. Nigel didn't want to dap fists, but saw Coach Shabaka looking in their direction. So to avoid a confrontation, he weakly bumped Denham's fist and walked away.

As players were leaving, Nigel came running back in. He had forgotten his favourite basketball. "Hey, Coach, forgot my —"

"Ball?" Coach Shabaka said holding it high.

"Ya, that's mine. That's the one you gave me last year."

"It's still in good condition. You're not using it enough."

"Ah, c'mon, Coach, you know that's not true. I play every day."

"You better."

Suddenly Denham appeared.

"Hey, Coach. You see my bag and stuff?" Denham asked.

"Hey, D," replied Coach Shabaka. "Ya, got your things right here."

Denham trotted toward Coach Shabaka and Nigel. "Sup, Nige. I mean Nigel," he said.

Nigel raised his chin and replied, "Yo."

"So, Denham, is your dad or mom outside, or are you still waiting?" asked Coach.

"I think Dad is supposed to come," said Denham. "He was supposed to bring me and then I guess he couldn't anymore. I'm not sure. I don't know who's coming for me, to be honest."

"All right. How about we call your mom quickly while we walk Nigel back out front, because it's getting late. Worse comes to worse, I'll drop you home. Is that cool?"

"Ya, Coach. That's cool. You have my mom's number, right?"

"Yes. I have it saved right here in my phone. Here, take it. The phone is ringing."

Denham gripped the phone close to his face. "Hi, Mom . . . Ya, I'm okay . . . No, Dad's not here . . . Uh huh. Okay. Well Coach said he could drop me . . . Uh huh . . . Okay, just a minute." He passed the phone back to Coach Shabaka. "Mom wants to speak to you."

Coach Shabaka took the phone. After speaking briefly with Denham's mother, he turned to Denham. "Your mother will be here soon, so let's go stand out in the lobby where we can see her car when she comes. C'mon, Nigel. Your father's waiting, right?"

"Yup, he's out front," Nigel replied.

"I wanted to tell you both how proud I am of you and how you played. You boys really work well together. The better you two get to know each other and work together the better the team will be. Trust me."

Nigel just rolled his eyes. He didn't want to acknowledge the collaboration that Coach Shabaka was excited about.

Denham's mother pulled up as soon as they entered the lobby. They walked outside to meet her. Nigel's father was parked ahead of her.

"Hey, Nigel, I want to talk to your father if he's not in a hurry," said Coach Shabaka. "Let me say hi to Denham's mother."

"Okay. I'll tell him." Leaning against the passenger side of his parents' car, Nigel spoke to his father through the window. He tried to hear what was going on with Coach and Denham's mom.

"I just get so frustrated with his father," Denham's mom was saying. "He was supposed to drop him to the game. He promised. He said he was going to stay and watch the whole game, and where is he? Not here. That's where. Now he can't even get here to pick the boy up. I just don't understand."

Nigel listened carefully to Denham's mother without letting anyone know he was eavesdropping. *Sounds like trouble in paradise*, Nigel thought, giggling to himself. *Sounds like his parents really don't get along. Sounds like his father don't care about him. Too bad.*

That moment, Denham's dad pulled up behind and hopped out of his car. "Hey, Coach. Sorry I'm late, brother. Where's D at? I'll take him home."

Coach Shabaka pointed to the back seat of the car

where Denham was sitting.

"Denham, go with your father," said Denham's mother.

"No," argued Denham's father. "He's already in your car."

"Oh. So you can go back to wherever you came from!"

"Don't start again!"

Denham's parents screamed at each other, unaware of all the people walking in and out of the gym, watching the argument. Nigel looked at Denham in the back seat. He smiled devilishly as Denham's hands covered his ears, and he closed his eyes, clearly wishing he was anywhere else.

13 I Got Something TO TELL YOU

The players arrived one by one and began taking warm-up shots. It was getting close to time to begin practice and Denham hadn't appeared yet. Coach Shabaka motioned to Coach Rodney to get practice started. Coach Rodney blew the whistle and gathered the players together.

This week it was Amritpal's turn to lead warm-up and stretches. They began with a light jog around the court in single file, following Amritpal. They then met at centre court to do jumping jacks, burpees and skipping without skipping ropes. After that, they began stretching their legs first, then arms and lower back. Coach Shabaka said it was important to stretch your muscles so that they would be loose and prevent injury while playing. After the stretches, Coach Shabaka gave them a quick talk about the last game and what they needed to improve on for next week's match.

"So today, boys, we're going to get started with some dribbling drills. I need you to find a partner and stand on the baseline with your balls, facing each other. The one standing on the baseline should have both basketballs."

They were short one player, so Kiya stepped in to substitute. She partnered with Nigel for the drill, which required him to dribble both balls at the same time toward the opposite baseline.

"Hey, Nige," Kiya said while walking backward, shadowing Nigel. "Dad's been acting weird lately. I think it has something to do with one of the players on this team. Acting like he's really worried. What did you guys do? Anyone get in trouble?"

They reached the opposite baseline and switched. Kiya was now the dribbler and Nigel walked backward. "Nah. Not that I can think of," Nigel replied. "But I do have something I gotta tell you."

"All right. What is it?" Kiya said.

"Not now. Not here. Maybe after practice. Confidential information. You need to hear this."

"Ohhhhh. Well, okay," Kiya said, shrugging.

Just as Coach Rodney sounded the whistle to begin the next drill, Denham came running in by himself, no mother and no siblings. "Hey, Coach, sorry I'm late," Denham said rushing to the bench to change into his basketball sneakers.

Coach Shabaka seemed happy to see him. Nigel was also happy to see Denham, but for a different reason. Nigel had come up with a new plan, one that might hurt Denham's feelings even more than Plan No-Pass. He knew just who to ask to help him out. Kiya would be the perfect partner in crime. Nigel thought about how heartbroken Denham might feel about his parents' separation, and it made Nigel smile. *Heartbroken, that's it. If I could find someone to pretend to like him and then break up with him just as he starts to really like her, he'll be devastated. Then when we reveal that it was all just a trap to make him like her, he'll never want to show his face around here again.*

"Hurry up now, Denham," said Coach Shabaka. "You got some catching up to do. Coach Rodney will be your partner for this drill."

The team dribbled both balls at the same time to begin, then switched to alternating right-hand and left-hand dribbles. Slow at first, then faster. They crouched and walked, doing low dribbles, then stood tall for high dribbles.

In the next drill, the players had to dribble with one hand and give their partner a high-five with the other, then switch hands when Coach Shabaka blew the whistle. Coach Shabaka then gave each pair a tennis ball and instructed them to keep dribbling with one hand and pass the tennis ball back and forth to each other with the other hand. When the players first began this drill, tennis balls were bouncing everywhere around the gym. But as they continued, the players were able to maintain control, carefully passing and catching the tennis ball while still dribbling. After the tennis ball drill, Coach Shabaka had them practise figure-eight dribbles around their legs and behind their backs. The players caught on to the techniques quickly.

"All right, well done, guys. Let's take a two-minute water break," said Coach Shabaka.

Most of the boys sprinted to the benches for a quick sip from their water bottles, then ran back out to the court to throw up more shots before Coach Shabaka resumed practice. Kiya did the same, and was about to practise her free throws when Nigel waved at her to follow him out of the gym to the water fountain.

"I'm not thirsty," Kiya said. "Besides, I have a water bottle at the bench, and so do you. What do we need to go out there for?"

"Just come," said Nigel. "Remember, I got something to tell you. C'mon."

14 New Plan, SAME GOAL

"You got something to tell me? Ya, ya, right. Let's go," Kiya said, and followed Nigel out of the gym. "Okay, Nigel, I'm here. What's up? Are you going to try to ask me out? If so, don't. You're like my little brother."

Her comment stunned Nigel for a moment. Although asking her out wasn't his intent, he did like her more than he wanted to admit to himself. "What? No. Don't be crazy. No, this is completely different."

"Okay, then, spit it out. What you want to tell me?"

"So I have a problem and I need your help."

"Are you in some sort of trouble, Nige? You know I got your back. How can I help?"

"The new guy on the team, Denham. I've got a problem with him."

"Really? He seems like a nice guy."

"He might seem nice, but sometimes the eyes lie, right?"

"Ya, ya of course, that's right. The eyes can lie. Okay, so what did he do?"

"He did me dirty, yo! He was bullying me, calling me fat, and lard butt, and pudgy boy. Then he was trying to punk me. I think he's going to try to beat me up."

Nigel exaggerated the truth. He really didn't want to lie, but he figured it would be the best way to get Kiya on board with his plan.

It worked. Kiya wanted to make Denham pay for what she thought he did to Nigel. "Yo. He can't do that," she said. "Yo, let's tell Dad and get him kicked off the squad. We don't need nobody like that here."

"Nah, nah, I got a better idea. Let's do this. How about you pretend that you like him. Pretend that you're going to be his girlfriend. Then you break his heart. Make him feel the pain, like how I felt when he was teasing me. Then we tell your father about what he did to me and get him kicked off the squad."

"I don't know, Nigel. Pretend to like someone that I don't have feelings for? That's dishonest. And isn't it kind of bullying too?"

"Yo, Kiya. He deserves it. Don't worry. An eye for an eye. It says that in the Bible, right? He got to pay the same way. He got to hurt the same way we're hurting right now. Trust me. This is the best payback."

"Nige. Nigel. I don't think I like this . . ." Kiya said with a sigh. "But if he's as bad as you say he is, you know I got your back, fam."

Nigel and Kiya returned to the gym with payback on their minds. Kiya didn't waste a second. She headed straight for Coach Rodney. "Hey, Coach. Can you do me a favour? Please, pretty please."

"Sure, little lady, anything for you."

"Could you switch partners with me? Nigel is starting to get on my nerves. Know what I'm saying?"

Coach Rodney broke out laughing. "Oh, ya, boys can do that sometimes. They can be a little immature. No problem. You partner with Denham. He's a good kid and you can definitely teach him a few things."

"Oh, I plan to," said Kiya. "Thanks, Coach."

The whistle blew and Coach Shabaka told the team they were going to do some defensive drills. The first was one he called the goalie drill. For each pair of players, pylons were set on the floor like a small soccer or hockey goal. One player would have the ball while the other would act like a goalie. The object of the game was for the player with the ball to dribble between the pylons. They could do crossover dribbles, fakes and anything that would help them get by the goalie. The goalie's job was to shuffle their feet side to side as quickly as possible and prevent the player with the ball from dribbling through the goal. If the defender stole the ball, they would get a point. If the offensive player dribbled between the pylons, they would get a point. The first one to get three points was the winner.

Kiya walked over to Denham and tossed her ball at his chest. "Hey, Denham, you got me for a partner now. Heads–up. You get first ball."

"Ummm, okay?" Denham replied. "You take it easy on me, now. I've seen how dangerous you are," he joked.

"Stop yapping and let's play," she barked.

Nigel smiled wickedly as he watched Kiya begin to set up the trap for Denham. *Nothing like a friendly game of love and basketball. All she's got to do is to get close enough to make him believe that she's interested. Then we got him!* Nigel thought.

Kiya stole the ball to win the first point. Denham did a double crossover and a spin through the pylons to win the second point. On the third point, Kiya beat Denham to the spot, Denham lost control of the ball and stumbled forward, only catching himself when his nose touched Kiya's nose. When Denham realized how close he was to her face, he jumped back and apologized.

"That's it! That's perfect, Kiya," Nigel whispered, keeping an eye on the two while doing the drill with Coach Rodney.

"Oh, it's okay, sweetie. I don't mind," Kiya said, seeing Denham's embarrassment. She knew she had caught his interest. Kiya looked over at Nigel and winked. Nigel responded with a nod. *Perfect start to the plan*, Nigel thought.

★★★

The coaches were cleaning up after practice and most of the boys had already been picked up by their parents. Nigel and Omari were taking shots on one side of the court. At the opposite basket, Kiya was still working her magic on Denham. Nigel watched them exchange affectionate glances.

"Yo, you see that," Nigel said to Omari.

"Ya. Dude. Are they in love now? She could do so much better. What's that about?"

"It's my new plan," Nigel said with pride. "Kiya is working with us. It's all part of the trap. She don't really like him. She's pretending. Then, when he asks if she could be his girlfriend, she's gonna drop him like a boulder and break his heart into a million pieces. Oh, I can't wait!"

"Yo. You are like . . . like an evil mastermind. I love it!" Omari gave Nigel a high-five.

Kiya smiled extra big at Denham as they passed the ball back and forth. "I wish we could stay here longer, D. This is nice. Y'know, hanging out with you. Is your mom coming soon?"

"Ya, this is cool," Denham agreed. "My moms is probably outside right now. I'm gonna check."

"Well, hold up, I'll go with you. If she's not there yet we could hang in the lobby a little longer and wait for her," Kiya said with a sneaky smile. It was a perfect chance to put the plan in fast forward.

Nigel spotted Kiya walking out with Denham

and tossed the ball to Omari. "Yo. I'll be right back. Gonna follow those two and see her work the plan some more," he said.

Kiya and Denham walked into the lobby toward the entrance. Nigel crept behind them, staying out of sight, watching and listening to them from a distance.

"So, Denham, aren't you going to ask me?" Kiya said.

"Huh? Ask you what?"

"If I have a boyfriend."

Denham was surprised and blushed a little.

"Well, don't worry," said Kiya. "I don't have one. So you can ask me for my number."

"I . . . can?"

"Yes, silly. Actually, give me your number and I'll call you."

Nigel could see that Denham was completely confused and wasn't sure what to do. Kiya pulled out a notebook and pencil from her purple gym bag. She told Denham to turn around and placed the notepad against his back for support. Then she insisted that he say his number aloud. Denham did so nervously.

Wow. Kiya is really believable, Nigel observed. *There's no way Denham will ever know what's going on. She even has me convinced, and I know she's pretending.*

When Kiya was finished, she put the notepad back in her bag and kissed Denham on the cheek. Kiya giggled, then pointed to the front door. "Is that your mother's van?"

"Uhhhh, I think so," Denham said.

"Kay. You better go. I'll call you later. Don't miss me too much."

Denham looked dazed and began to walk away as if he were hypnotized.

"Bye, D," Kiya said, giggling.

"Uh, buh . . . bye," Denham said and disappeared through the door.

Nigel approached as Kiya was still waving. "Didn't realize you were such a good actor, Key," he said.

"The best," she said, laughing. "The best."

5 I'll Do It MYSELF

The Power went on a ten-game winning streak to close out the season as first-place seed for the playoffs. Despite the success, Nigel was still holding his grudge against Denham. And now he was starting to feel jealous about all the time Kiya was spending with Denham. He was getting impatient. He felt she should've dropped the bomb on him already, revealing that she didn't really like him, that it was all just a prank. Any time he tried to mention it to her, though, she would say she'd do it soon and put him off until later. So Nigel decided he would confront Kiya at practice and let her know it was time to proceed with the next phase of the plan.

Nigel was one of the first to show up for the warm-up. Coach Shabaka wasn't in the gym, but Nigel saw Kiya practising her step-back jumpshots. He darted over to where she was.

"Hey, Key, wassup," he said.

"Oh, hey there, Nige. You ready? You excited to start the playoffs? I think we're gonna mash it up!

Other teams better watch out. Yo, you and Denham are hard to beat when you work together. No other team has a backcourt that can compare to you guys."

"That's kinda what I want to talk to you about," Nigel said, lowering his voice to a whisper. "So when we going to let Denham know this was all a prank and get him off the team?"

Kiya put her ball on the floor, sat on it and motioned for Nigel to do the same. "Dude, the playoffs start next week," she said. "So much time has passed. You really still on that? Listen, Nigel. I don't want to tell Denham it's a prank anymore. I know you're mad about what Denham did. But I don't think you need to be upset about that any longer. After talking with him, I can tell you, he's not so bad. I kinda like him. He's actually cool . . . and you guys play so good together."

Nigel rolled his eyes.

Kiya continued, "I'm not saying that he didn't do anything wrong to you. Maybe he did, but can't you let it go? Believe it or not, he told me that he respects you and is impressed by your leadership. He says he wishes that he was as strong as you on the court. He loves sharing the backcourt with you."

That surprised Nigel. For the first time, he lost his focus on revenge. For just a moment, he wondered if he had taken his revenge too far. "But what about all his fat talk, yo? That's not respecting me."

"Ya, he said he did that mostly because he didn't

know how to connect with you. He thought he could joke around with you. I dunno, I guess cuz that's what guys do? He was wrong, no doubt. Look, you guys need to talk so you both can understand where the other is coming from. I think you guys make a good team. That's why I abandoned the plan weeks ago."

Hearing that Kiya had ditched his plan infuriated Nigel all over again. "Weeks ago?! So you've been pretending to pretend all this time?!"

"Nigel, you have the best record in the league. You're about to start the playoffs and you have a chance to win it all. You should be happy. Why would you want to throw one of the best players off the team and throw that all away now? Why not forgive him? Maybe even become his friend?"

"Friend!" Nigel said, almost yelling. "I'm not looking for any new friends. I thought you were my friend, but I guess I was wrong. You were supposed to have my back. I can't believe you'd sell me out like this. You sound as if you and he really have something going on."

"Sell you out? Look, Nigel, I'm sorry. I did agree to your plan at first. But that was a mistake. As time passed, I was, like, what is the point of this? What am I doing? Trying to hurt someone's feelings because he might've hurt your feelings? It's not right, Nigel. Plus you're holding on to this grudge for so long and only god knows why. Oh, and for the record, it's no business of yours who I do or do not have something going with. Understand? Really, what is your problem with Denham?"

"You're supposed be on my team, Kiya, not his. This was our payback plan. Not a love connection. Just forget it. I'll take care of this myself. I don't need your help. I don't need nobody's help. All of you are sell outs!"

Nigel jumped to his feet and kicked the basketball that he was sitting on toward the corner. The ball ricocheted off both walls and sailed back in Nigel's direction. He caught the ball and began shooting jumpshots at the nearest basket.

Once all the players arrived, Coach Shabaka rallied the boys together. "All right, everyone, let's get practice started. No fooling around today. As you may have noticed, Coach Rodney is absent. He's a little under the weather, so he won't be joining us. We hope he has a speedy recovery. So you guys just got me today. Oh, yes, and Kiya too, of course. So Coach Rodney made me promise that you guys do one thing today . . ."

"What's that, Coach?" Nigel asked.

"Coach Rodney said he'd feel absolutely terrible if you had an easy practice today. He said we've done a great job the last few weeks. But he doesn't want you guys to get lazy or take our wins for granted, so he wants us to run hard today. Start earning next Saturday's win by putting in the work now. So everybody up, balls stay on the ground. Get into defensive stance, feet shoulder-width apart, bend your knees, get low and run on the spot. Let's go! Keep those feet moving!"

All the sneakers tapping the floor sounded like a stampede. The boys galloped as Coach Shabaka hollered out instructions.

"Drop to the floor and do a push-up when I lower my arm. And . . . let's go!"

The boys dropped, pushed up and sprang to their feet.

"Next. Shuffle to the right. Keep those feet moving. Now shuffle left. Back to the right. Drop and gimme five push-ups. Back on your feet. Defensive stance. Keep running on the spot. Let's do it all again."

The boys were drenched with sweat and this was only the beginning. Coach Shabaka continued an intense practice with more drills, a lot of running and repetition of their plays. He split them into two teams for scrimmage. Team one was Nigel, Omari, Kash, Amritpal and Mohammad, against team two, which was Denham, Amen, Sundeep, Asim and Tony.

"All right, boys, let me get two of you for the jump ball," called out Coach Shabaka. "I'm going to referee with Kiya today. We're not going to make a lot of calls, so be sure to play through contact. Don't complain about getting fouled because, if a referee misses the call this Saturday in the playoff game, they will give you a technical foul if you start whining. It's all a part of being mentally tough. Do your best to take a hit and still score the basket. Okay, let's go!"

16 PAYBACK

The boys played fierce in the scrimmage and began to trash talk each other after blocked shots and made baskets. Denham and Nigel were covering each other. In one series, Nigel pulled up for a jumpshot and drained it over top of Denham's outstretched hand.

"Eat that!" Nigel said, jogging backward to his end of the court.

Not to be outdone, Denham came down the court. He drove directly at Nigel, then stopped suddenly, leaving Nigel stumbling. Denham crossed the ball between his legs to the left, then crossed it behind his back to his right and drove to the net. Nigel recovered, but not quickly enough. He fouled Denham across his arm as he laid the ball in. As Coach Shabaka had warned, he let the foul go and didn't blow the whistle.

"And one!" Denham yelled. Then, as he jogged by Nigel, he murmured, "You know you can't guard me, tubby baby. You never could. Not yesterday, not today, not ever."

Payback

Nigel started to bubble with anger. He became reckless with the ball and tried to go straight back at Denham. He forgot his teammates as if he and Denham were playing one-on-one. Nigel tried his own crossover dribble, but Denham poked the ball away. Nigel got the ball back and tried again. This time he tried to crossover and do a spin move toward the basket, but Denham wasn't fooled by the move. He waited for Nigel to rise, then slapped Nigel's shot out of the air and out of bounds. Denham wagged his index finger in Nigel's direction saying, "No, no, no." He laughed as Nigel went to recover the ball.

Nigel's anger continued to grow. He clenched his fists before he picked up the ball to pass it inbounds.

"Hold on there, boys," Coach Shabaka said, removing his phone from his pocket. "I've got a call. I'm going to take this in the hallway. Kiya, you keep the game going. I'll be right back."

"Sure thing, Dad," Kiya said, and blew the whistle to restart the game.

Nigel stood out of bounds, looking for an open player to throw the inbound pass to. Denham stood face to face with Nigel, hands out, trying to block Nigel's vision.

"You might as well just give me the ball now," said Denham with a smirk. "Because the next time you touch it it'll be a turnover. I'm going to take it from you like taking candy from a big fat baby." He patted Nigel on his belly.

Nigel's anger was near maximum level now. He wanted to throw the ball at Denham. He wanted to smoosh his face with it and laugh at Denham rolling on the floor in pain.

Kiya said, "Come on, Nigel, five-second count. You got to toss the ball in."

Nigel held the ball behind his head as if he was about to do a soccer throw-in. Then he faked a pass right into Denham's face.

"No, Nigel. Don't!" Kiya screamed.

Denham flinched as the ball grazed his cheekbone.

"What's that for!" Denham yelled, knocking the basketball out of Nigel's hands. "It's just a game. You trying to throw hands over this? What's your problem, yo?"

"You're my problem."

"So what you going to do about it? You really acting like a big pudgy baby now. Let's just finish the game."

"I ain't playing no more. I don't want you on this team. No one does."

"Nigel, stop," yelled Kiya. She tried to get in between the boys.

The other players crowded around them as Nigel continued. "No one here likes you. They're all pretending. Kash don't like you. He's pretending. Omari hates you. Asim, Amritpal and Tony, they pretending too. They don't like you. Even Kiya is pretending. She never liked you and she never will."

Denham looked around at the other Power players. They all dropped their heads and wouldn't look him in the eye. He looked at Kiya. She was shaking her head. Her eyes were pleading with Nigel to stop.

"Notice in the beginning no one was passing the ball to you," Nigel drove on. "Thought it was strange, didn't you! Wasn't no accident. That was cuz of me. I told everyone not to pass to you. But then Coach got in the way of that. We never wanted you on this team. Not even your parents like you. Your father never wants to come for you. I bet he doesn't want you either, and your moms has no time for you. She don't even want to watch you play. You're just a stupid reject. I saw when they were arguing outside the other day. None of them wanted to take you. They getting divorced and neither of them wants to keep you. They going to turn you over to the homeless kids' shelter. No one wants you."

Denham lunged at Nigel and grabbed him by his neck. The two boys scuffled on the ground, rolling around as the other players jumped in, trying to separate them. Coach Shabaka ran back into the gym, drawn by the commotion. "What's going on here?!" he yelled. He wrestled the boys apart. "That's enough! You two, to the bench now! Cool off. The rest of you. Play four on four. Kiya get them started."

Kiya nodded nervously as she watched Nigel and

Denham stomp to the bench. They sat on opposite sides while Coach Shabaka spoke to them.

"I don't want to know what happened or who started it. None of that," said Coach Shabaka, shaking his head. "I'm going to tell you guys one thing. You are teammates. This team is a family. You don't have to like your family, but you do have to work together. I'm not going to force you to apologize. We're just going to pound it out. So come closer, raise your fists, give each other a pound, look each other in the eye and say, 'Family.' Done."

The boys did it reluctantly. Coach Shabaka left them on the bench with a warning that if they started fighting again, they would be banned from playing the playoff game on Saturday. Nigel and Denham went back to sitting on opposite sides of the bench and didn't say another word.

7 Run Out THE CLOCK

For the last game of the regular season, the Power had celebrated a big blowout win by more than thirty points against the Wildcats. The two teams were set to play each other again for the first game of the playoffs.

Coach Shabaka warned the team that this time would not be so easy. "It's hard to beat the same team twice in a row, back-to-back weeks. Especially if they were embarrassed the last game. They are going to come out swinging, and we have to be prepared to absorb their attack. Amen and Asim, you guys dominated the paint last week. Let's do more of that. Then, when they try to double team you down low, kick the ball out to one of the wing players. Kash, Nigel, Denham, keep that ball moving around the perimeter and take advantage when their defence is a step slow. Most importantly, boys, let's work together."

Nigel and Denham looked at each other and scowled. They knew that Coach Shabaka was specifically referring to them.

"All right, boys. It's that time. This is the first stop on our road to the championship. Let's make it count. Hands in. I HAVE THE . . ."

The players surprised Coach Shabaka, as they had orchestrated a call and response where half of them yelled, "POWER!" and the other half hollered it back even louder. They did it twice so it sounded like an enthusiastic echo that shook the walls of the gym.

The Power used that energy and broke out to a quick 12–0 lead. Amen and Asim scored all of the points, as they overpowered the smaller Wildcat players. But it was too easy a start, and the Power naturally began to relax. The Wildcats coach called a timeout to get his team to regain their focus. They did. They closed the quarter on a 25–5 run to take a 25–17 lead.

Although they didn't have the height that the Power had, the Wildcats had speed. They were outrunning and out-hustling the Power players in all aspects. Before they knew it, the Power were down 43–21 at the half.

As the Power players huddled together, Nigel knew just what Coach Shabaka was going to say — "Basketball is a game of runs." Nigel knew it was time for him to spearhead a run to get the Power back into the game. He had laser focus as the second half got under way. He went on a personal 10–0 run, hitting jumpshots as if he were throwing the ball into the ocean. He couldn't miss. Nigel's aggressive play seemed to spark Denham, who scored twelve straight points off of steals, layups and three-pointers, to close the gap between the Wildcats and the Power. It almost seemed as if Nigel and Denham were playing against each other, each one trying to outdo the other. They both did an excellent job setting up teammates for open shots, but did not pass the ball to each other. Despite that, they managed to keep the score close.

In the fourth quarter, the Power and the Wildcats continued to trade baskets, taking the lead then giving it up the next trip down the court. It was a real tug-of-war. The Power were down by two points by the time there was less than a minute left on the clock. They were getting anxious because their season was in jeopardy.

The Wildcats had possession of the ball after Kash fumbled a pass from Denham out of bounds. Coach Shabaka subbed Omari in for Asim to provide better on-ball defence. He whispered to Omari to tell the other players to trap the Wildcats player who would catch the inbound pass. As soon as the ball was inbounded, Omari and Denham pounced on the man with the ball. He got rattled and coughed up the rock. Omari tipped it toward Nigel who was racing ahead, followed by three Wildcat players. Nigel leaped sky high to grab the loose ball, but was surrounded by Wildcats as he came down with it. Out of the corner of his eye, he spotted Denham with his hands open, ready to receive the pass. But Nigel wasn't about to pass away this moment. Especially not to Denham. Nigel took a few dribbles closer to the three-point line and pulled up for the jumper with hands in his face.

SPLASH! Nigel's shot was wetter than leaves in a rainforest.

The Wildcats coach signalled for a timeout as the referee raised her arms to indicate the three-pointer was good. After the timeout, the Wildcats wanted to hurl a pass down the court. Instead, the Wildcats player tossed it too high, out of reach and directly out of bounds. Turnover. It was the Power's ball. All they had to do was to run out the clock and the game would be over. The Wildcats coach called his last timeout.

8 No, No, I GOT IT

There were ten seconds on the clock, with the Power leading by one. Coach Shabaka drew up an inbounds play — Amen would pass the ball to Nigel in the back-court so he could get fouled or dribble out the clock. Nigel was the best ball handler and best free-throw shooter on the team. Every player understood their role.

The Power players all got into position on the court. Amen was stationed out of bounds at the half-court line, waiting for the referee to hand over the ball. The referee blew the whistle, dropped the ball into Amen's hands and began the five-second count. Nigel tried to shake free of the Wildcats defenders, but they were stuck like glue to him. No one else could get free either. With one second left on the referee's count, Amen lobbed a pass in Nigel's direction, hoping that he would jump and secure the possession. Instead, one the Wildcats players tipped the pass, and the ball bounced onto the Power's side of the court, closer to where Denham was. Nigel raced to retrieve the ball ahead of the Wildcats players. Denham also took off, trying to secure the rock. They scooped up the ball at the same time. Nigel and Denham wrestled for the ball, each gripping it with two hands. Both tried to secure the win by ripping it away from the other.

"Let go! Give it to me. Let them foul me," Nigel demanded as the Wildcats defenders inched toward them.

"It's okay. It's okay. No, I got it," Denham replied.

"Just let go!" Nigel cried. He used all his force and body weight to snatch the ball away. The sudden yank made Denham go off balance, twisting his ankle and dropping him hard to the floor. Nigel lost control and the ball squirted out of his hands, right into the hands of the nearest Wildcats player. With seconds left on the clock, the Wildcats player pulled up for the game-winning shot.

BAAAAP!

The shot was blocked from behind by Kash, who had sprinted down the court in time to get a hand on the ball. The buzzer sounded to end the game as time expired.

TWEET! TWEET! Both referees blew their whistles, indicating there was a foul on the play. The Power players tried to protest, until they realized that Denham was still rolling on the floor in pain, gripping his ankle. Coach Shabaka hurried out onto the court to attend to Denham. Nigel was in complete shock. He couldn't believe what happened, that they had given the Wildcats a chance to tie or win the game. His first thought was to blame Denham. If Denham had just let go of the ball, none of this would have happened. However, now that he saw Denham rocking in pain on the floor, Nigel couldn't help but feel bad. He had to realize that it wasn't all Denham's fault.

Coach Shabaka and Amen helped Denham to his feet and served as his crutches because Denham couldn't put any pressure on the hurt ankle. Kiya and Coach Rodney ran off to get ice packs and the first aid kit for Denham's quickly swelling ankle, while the referees cleared the court so that the Wildcats could take their final free throws. The referee indicated that there were to be three shots because the player was behind the three-point line when he was fouled in the act of shooting.

Nigel dropped to his knees, hands on his head in disbelief that the Wildcats would have three chances to at least tie the game. The Wildcats player stepped to the free-throw line. He looked nervous. He stood straight-legged and, with shaky hands, he threw up the first shot. It banged against the backboard and bounced off the front of the rim. The Power players breathed a slight sigh of relief, but didn't celebrate. The Wildcats still had two more shots. The Wildcats player walked away from the free-throw line to shake out his jitters. He returned to the line with renewed confidence. This time he bent his knees and allowed the ball to roll off his shooting hand. Again the ball hit the backboard hard, but this time the backspin forced it to drop directly into the basket.

The Power players moaned. The Wildcats clapped, but not too much, because they knew it wasn't over yet. One more made free throw would win them the game. A miss meant they were going to overtime.

Nigel was still on his knees, praying for a miss. He vowed to win the game if he got another chance to play. He just needed the Wildcats to miss the free throw. The Wildcats player at the line took a deep breath as the referee tossed him the ball and signalled that he could take the shot. The gym went completely silent. The Wildcats player held the ball at his hip while simulating the shot with his free hand. He then took hold of the ball with both hands, bent his knees, took aim and released the ball from his hands in what looked like slow motion. The players were all held captive by the floating pumpkin. The orange ball hit the back of the orange rim and bounced high above the backboard before nestling on the front of the rim. Players from both teams and spectators all gasped, unable to tell whether the ball was going to fall in or fall out.

Nigel jumped to his feet in excitement. "PLEASE!" he whispered loudly, holding his fists high in the air. The ball teetered forward and back like a seesaw, before finally falling through the net. The Wildcats and their fans exploded with cheers. Nigel and the rest of the Power players were devastated. Their season was over with a loss in the first round of the playoffs. It was a major upset — the first-place team losing to the lowest seed in the playoffs. And Nigel had to wonder if his plans against Denham had anything to do with it.

19 Not My FAULT

The teams lined up to shake hands at centre court, except Denham, who was getting his leg wrapped with a tensor bandage and ice pack by Coach Rodney and Kiya. The Wildcats showed great sportsmanship and respect. Each went to the Power bench to slap hands with Denham and wish him well.

Coach Shabaka gathered the team together for one last talk before releasing them to their waiting parents. "Boys, it's a hard way to lose. You see how things can change in a game within a matter of seconds. And I have to say. All my years of coaching, I have never . . . never seen two players on the same team fighting for the ball in the middle of the game before. What is going on with you two?!"

"Coach, you said you wanted me to handle the ball at the end. Get fouled and take the free throws," said Nigel trying to defend himself.

"Sure, but never did I say to wrestle your teammate to the floor and sprain his ankle!"

Nigel hung his head as Coach Shabaka continued. "Denham, I'm sorry you got hurt, but you're not blameless either. Numerous times I've spoken to all of you about working together and showing respect for each other. Instead, we have an injured player and our season is over. Because we lacked unity. You boys will have a lot to think about during the off season. I'm disappointed. I am. But despite everything, I'm still proud of you. We've made some mistakes, sure. But we got this far because we worked hard. And for the most part, you worked together, even if it was reluctantly. Just keep this in mind, always. The more we work together, the farther we will go. Okay? Hands in."

The team threw their hands to the centre of the huddle one last time in the season to chant their name, "POWER." The players gathered their belongings and darted toward their parents.

Nigel watched Kiya, with Denham's mother and his siblings, help Denham to his feet. *I didn't mean to sprain his ankle. I mean, ya, I wanted to hurt him. But not like this*, Nigel thought. *Why did he grab the ball, when he knew I was supposed to be the one to finish the game for the team? It's his own fault that he got hurt.* Nigel tried to convince himself while Kiya strapped Denham's bag around her shoulder, and Denham's siblings grabbed his street kicks and water bottle. They stood on either side of him and he leaned on them for support.

After getting his balance, Denham looked up in

Nigel's direction. They stared angrily at each other for a few seconds. Then Denham shook his head in disgust and began hopping toward the front lobby. Seeing the difficulty that Denham was having even trying to stand up straight made Nigel feel uncomfortable about what had happened on the court. *Dag, he's hurt pretty bad. He can't even walk and I did that to him. But I told him to let go of the ball. He didn't listen. He decided to keep holding on to it. He tried to fight me for it. Now look what he did to himself. Really, ya, he hurt himself.*

Nigel watched a memory reel of events from the past year, trying to tell himself that he wasn't at fault. *During summer league he kept clowning me. Calling me "fat-boy baller." He called me a belly dancer! Then he comes on my team, talking about wanting to be a better leader. What kinda leadership is bullying and fat-shaming a kid like me? He wanted to take over my team. I wasn't about to let that happen. Not on my watch!*

Nigel remembered Denham's look of disappointment when he couldn't get a pass from the team. Nigel had been proud of that moment, but now he wasn't so sure. He realized Denham now wore the same look of helplessness at not being able to walk on his own. So different from that smug smile Nigel had wanted to wipe off of his face. *He deserves everything that has happened. I'm the victim, not him. Calling me tubby baby and laughing at me when he blocked my shot. He got what he deserved. So why do I feel so guilty about it? Why?*

Nigel gave his gym gear to his parents, told them that he would meet them at the car and went after Denham. He didn't know why, or what he was going to say, but he felt that he should say something. He caught up to the group but remained out of sight as they sat Denham on the cushioned benches in the front lobby. Denham's mother stroked her son's head and said, "I'm going to bring the car around. Kiya, you don't mind waiting here with him?"

"Not at all, Mrs. Dubois. Go ahead. I'll stay," replied Kiya.

Denham didn't look very enthused about Kiya remaining there with him. "Look, you ain't gotta stay. No need to pretend anymore. The season's over, so I guess you guys got what you wanted. And tell your father to make sure not to draft me for the Power next season."

"No, D, don't be like that," said Kiya. "I'm staying. How many times can I apologize? I was wrong. So wrong. Nigel told me about all this terrible stuff you did and I wanted to help him. Then when we got to be friends, I realized that he wasn't truthful about everything."

"Ya, whatevs," Denham said, shaking his head. "I'll be glad to be rid of both of you once I leave this place."

"That's not true, D. You don't mean that," Kiya said, tears forming in her eyes.

"Oh, yes, I do," said Denham.

20 We Are THE POWER

Nigel couldn't stay hidden anymore. "Nah, you don't mean that," he said to Denham. "It's not her fault."

"Oh, great," said Denham, trying to turn away from both of them. "You're here, too. Where's my moms? Ughh. I can't leave here fast enough. Besides you can't make anyone do anything that they don't want to do. So no excuses."

Kiya rose to her feet and pushed Nigel in the chest with both hands. "See what you did! You happy now?"

"I'm not. I messed up, Key. I know."

"What are you even doing here, Nigel?" Denham asked. "Can't you both just let me suffer in peace and go away! I don't get it, Nigel. Why? What did I ever do to you?"

"Whadda you mean! You been trying to punk me since summer league. We played your team, you kept talking about my weight and calling me names. It really got me heated. Then you joined our team and all I could think about was revenge. Plus, all your trash talk, it really got under my skin, yo."

"But that was just trash talk. It doesn't mean anything."

"It still made me mad, yo. I didn't like it at all. I don't like people calling me fat and you kept doing it. Over and over and . . ."

"That's cuz you are f —" Denham began. He stopped when he saw Nigel clenching his fists.

"See! That's exactly what I'm talking about," Nigel said through clenched teeth. "You think you could just talk reckless. Like it don't mean nothing. Like I'm a big joke. I ain't no joke. Just cuz I'm bulkier than you, you wanna make fun of me? So many times I wanted to pound your face into the ground. I can't lie. I still want to now."

"Well, is this enough revenge for you?" Denham asked, pointing down to his foot. "But I kinda get it. I guess I felt the same way when you talked about my folks. That was a low blow."

"No lower than what you did. Talking 'bout my weight is outta bounds."

"Really! Bruh. You was talking 'bout my moms, man. Everyone knows you don't do that. Moms is off limits. That made me wanna fight you. And if I wasn't injured, I'd slap you up, right here, right now."

There was an awkward silence. Kiya watched the boys sizing each other up, looking fiercely at each other. Denham's jaw clenched, as his lips curled into a snarl. Veins vibrated in Nigel's neck as his glare intensified.

"So, what, are you guys gonna fight now?" Kiya said. "This is going nowhere! Look, Denham, you're just as much at fault as the rest of us. You shouldn't have been clowning Nigel like that. What you did was mean. You can't be critical of us when you were acting like the bully first. I admit I should've known better. I messed up too. And Nigel, look what your payback has gotten you. You lost in the first round of the playoffs to the worst team. You lost the best player you've ever played with cuz you mashed up his ankle. You probably lost Dad's respect. And you might've lost me as a friend. Was it worth it? All your stupid plans!"

The awkward silence returned. All three just stared at each other.

"Sooooo are you guys gonna fight now, or what?" Kiya said jokingly, trying to lighten the mood.

All three frowned at one another. Then they broke out laughing.

"Shut up, Kiya. I'm still mad at you," Nigel snapped back, still laughing. "But you're right. I feel like I sabotaged everything. I shouldn't have lied to you and made you start hating on Denham."

"Exactly," said Kiya. "I'm almost like an innocent bystander in all of this. Besides, I've been the only one trying to talk sense into both of you this whole time."

"Okay, Kiya, you got a point," admitted Denham. "I wouldn't exactly say you're innocent but . . . Nigel, maybe I got a little carried away with all that fat stuff.

Y'know, I only did it cuz I needed to get an edge when playing against you. You're stronger and, though I hate to admit it, you're probably a better player than I am. I had to get into your head somehow to throw you off your game so I could win. Then, when I joined the Power, I guess I was kinda jealous of how all the guys looked up to you. I wish I could play as confidently as you do. It looks so easy for you. I mean, ya, you're kinda bulky, but you use that to your advantage. I wish I could power through people on the court the way you do."

"You're jealous of me and my size?"

"Ya, look how skinny I am, bro. I could hula hoop with a Cheerio, dude. I'm like a pinball on the court, always bouncing off other players. I need some more muscle, like you."

"Wow. For real?"

"For real, yo."

"I never looked at it that way. I've always been defensive when people talk about my size. But, Denham, it's true. You is kinda skinny, yo," Nigel laughed.

"Get outta here, Nige. I mean Nigel," Denham tried to correct himself.

"Nah, bruh, call me Nige. My friends call me Nige. Ain't that right, Key?"

Kiya smiled at them both. "Ya, Nige. We do. Hey, D. Ain't that your mother's ride right there?" Kiya said as she eyed Denham's mother's vehicle pulling up to the door.

"Yup, yup. That's her. Well, I guess if I don't forgive you guys and tell you to leave me alone, I'm going to have a hard time getting to my mom's car," said Denham. Kiya and Nigel chuckled at the joke.

"Yo, I'm . . . I'm sorry for everything," said Nigel. "Not just the ankle, but everything. It's my bad. Should've never gone this far."

"Ya, I know, man. I know. It's my bad too. For all the fat jokes and bagging on you all the time."

"What I should've done was just beat you down during summer league," Nigel said, grinning. "Would've been a lot less stress."

"Oh, you wish. C'mon, guys help me up," Denham said, chuckling. "Look, Kiya, I think you're cool and I want us to keep talking. You know, stay in contact. Plus, I'm going to need you to help me rehab and come back a stronger player than before. You are hands-down the best player I've ever gone against."

"Better believe I'll get you back in shape, D. You may never beat me one-on-one, but I can at least help you get close." Kiya smiled and rested her head against Denham's shoulder as they walked.

"Yo, and Nige," Denham said enthusiastically. "You know, we made a pretty good team when we worked together. We was fire this season and we didn't even like each other."

"Finished first place," Nigel replied.

"Right. We were the best and we didn't even try. So maybe summer ball, when my ankle has healed, we could really take over the league."

"Oh, ya. No doubt, bruh. We could run tings."

Denham's mother hopped out of the vehicle and hurried around to open the passenger door for Denham. Kiya and Nigel helped lower Denham into the car.

"Call me after you get home from the hospital. Let me know what the doctor says," Kiya said.

Denham nodded as she bent down to hug him.

"Ewwww. D's got a girlfriend," cried Denham's younger brothers from the back seat.

"Be quiet back there," Denham said, laughing. He turned his attention toward Nigel and held his hand out.

Nigel reached into the car, slapping and sliding his hand against Denham's until their fingers locked together to make a power fist.

"Power, bruh," Denham said.

"Ya. Power," Nigel said. "We are the Power."

Epilogue
THUNDER AND LIGHTNING

It was midsummer, and Kiya was giving extra coaching to Nigel and Denham, preparing them for the summer league championship. Dripping with sweat, the two boys took turns zigzagging through fluorescent orange pylons, finishing with jumpshots and layups.

"Let's pick it up, guys!" yelled Kiya, as Nigel and Denham raced from baseline to baseline. "We can't afford to take these guys lightly. That's it!" Kiya yelled, hitting the button on her stopwatch. "Yo, D, you did that two seconds faster than last run. Hard to believe that you had busted your ankle."

"Ya, bruh," said Nigel, trying to catch his breath. "It's like you got faster after your rehab."

"Guess I should thank you for that, Nige," Denham said, huffing and chuckling at the same time.

"Aw, man, don't even play me like that, yo," Nigel replied.

The three kids leaned against each other, trying to prop themselves up while enjoying the joke.

"But for real, D," said Kiya. "You move like . . . like lightning on the court."

"Well, if I'm lightning, what's Nigel?"

"Hmmm. Nige is fast but not as fast as you. He's got that power game."

"Ya, pure muscle going hard in the paint," Denham said.

Nigel flexed his arms, growled and made a stink face that made the other two break out laughing again.

"Got it," Kiya said. "If D is lightning then Nigel is thunder. Ya. You guys are Thunder and Lightning."

"I kinda like that," Nigel said, nodding. "Ya, that's cool. But what about you? You gotta be . . . you gotta be Rain, cuz of the way you rain threes on everyone."

Denham jumped in. "Or, yo, she can be Rainbow cuz of the high arc her shot takes before it splashes in the pot of gold. She almost hits the roof when she shoots."

"Okay, okay," said Kiya, laughing. "Not mad at that. Thunder, Lightning and the Rainbow. Sounds like a singing group."

"Forget singing. We should enter the three-on-three tournament at the end of summer," Nigel exclaimed.

"True, I'm with that," Kiya said. "But, yo, that's for later. Let's stay focused on now. We got a championship to win tomorrow. Let's work. Pick and rolls now! Let's get it."

Half-Court Trap

***

Game day of the Brampton summer league finals featured the Vipers versus the Power. Both teams were playing lights-out, undefeated for the last fifteen games. It was an epic matchup of all-star duos. The Vipers' Ezekial Mutat and Kadeem Brown against the Power's Denham Dubois and Nigel Barnes.

Coach Shabaka gathered the team together for their pregame chant. "Okay, let's go out there and prove what you have been showing teams all season. That we're the best at working together. Fists in . . ."

The Power players replied, "Yes, yes. That's right," while layering their fists one on top of the other over Coach Shabaka's.

Nigel and Denham nodded at each other, then over at Kiya. She was on her toes, reaching with both fists to top the mountain of hands.

"You guys remember, right?" Kiya said. "THE MORE WE WORK TOGETHER . . ."

The Power boys responded in chorus, ". . . THE FARTHER WE WILL GO!!!!"

"That's right," Coach Shabaka said. "All right, everyone. Together on three. One-two-three."

"TOGETHER!!!"

The Power players ran onto the court with a look of determination, high-fiving each other and repeating, "TOGETHER. TOGETHER," with each hand slap.

They shook hands with the opposing team and took their positions for the jump ball. The referee tossed the orange globe in the air and the game was on.

The Power started with possession. They spread the court, scattering the Vipers defence so that each player got a touch before finding an open shot. Denham and Nigel worked their pick and rolls to perfection, allowing Kash, Amen and Amritpal to score easily. When Tony and Omari entered the game, they followed Nigel and Denham in continuing to distribute the ball, getting scores for Sundeep, Mohammed and Asim. The whole Power team was contributing, but they still had a difficult time containing the Vipers star backcourt Ezekial and Kadeem. At the half the score was 47–47.

"C'mon, boys, we need to buckle down and pick up our defensive intensity," said Coach Shabaka during his half-time speech. "Those two boys are shredding our defence. Stay disciplined. Move your feet! Don't let them penetrate the paint. Force them to take long shots. All right, let's go!"

The Vipers and the Power traded punches like heavyweight boxers. Neither let the other get a lead more than three. Then a turnover gave the Vipers a four-point lead with thirty seconds left on the clock.

Coach Shabaka called a timeout. "All right, boys. We need two baskets and a defensive stop to, at least, tie the game. No more turnovers. Denham, I want you to run some action on Kash's side. Everyone set screens to loosen the defence. Soon as we score, full-court press. Okay, let's do it!"

The Power boys were nervous, afraid the championship might slip through their fingers. Nigel put his arm around Denham and said, "D, we need your speed right here. Get to your spot, yo. We need this!"

Denham nodded, taking the inbound pass. Ezekial defended him full court to kill time on the clock. Denham zigzagged, trying to shake the pressure. He flipped the pass to Nigel, then cut baseline. Nigel pitched it right back.

Defenders tried to barricade, but Denham was pure finesse. He slid into the key between defenders like butter, and finished with a silky finger roll that had spectators hollering, "Ooooooooh."

The Power were down by just two points. They picked up full court. Kadeem tried to inbound to Ezekial. Denham intercepted the ball, knowing exactly where it was going. Both teams were scrambling. Denham was surrounded by Vipers, but spotted Nigel in the corner. He quickly vaulted a pass to him. Nigel stood at the three-point line, poised to shoot a three to win. His defender closed in, but flew by as Nigel put up a shot fake. With seconds left on the clock, Nigel launched himself toward the rim. Vipers players collided into Nigel as he released a layup off the glass. "Count it. And one!" the referee yelled as time expired. Nigel landed, flexing both arms, roaring like a lion. The Power players surrounded him, jumping in celebration.

The referees quickly cleared the court for Nigel to shoot the final free throw. Nigel approached the line, adrenaline still pumping. He knew if he didn't calm down, he would overshoot the basket.

"You got this, bro," said Denham. "We are the Power. Remember that. Everything we've gone through, yo, we boys for life."

"For life," Nigel repeated as they pounded fists. Nigel thought about the past year. It was exactly a year ago that he and Denham began their feud. After all the anger and resentment, today they were united, cheering each other on. He looked down at his stocky legs, his chunky arms, his belly hanging over the waist of his basketball shorts — and smiled. Nigel had learned to love the advantages that being bigger afforded him. He took a deep breath, patted his belly and took the shot . . .

SWISH!

ACKNOWLEDGEMENTS

Thank you to my family, my wife, Nicolia and son Tyce. My sister, Sheena, and my parents Jemima and Listford Jones. Thank you for encouraging me to read when I thought I hated it.

Thanks to my brother from another: Francis McLean and family; Julie Corona, Celia, Joaquin and Amina.

Thanks to the Brampton Minor Basketball Association — The first house league I ever played in and gained confidence in as a player, then later gained confidence as a coach. Thank you!

To the Milton Stags Basketball Club — Thank you for allowing me to coach, to inspire and to be inspired by the youth who have played in the leagues.

To all the coaches I had throughout my lifetime in every sport, your energy and tutelage were invaluable to my development and to the values I live by now.

To my Knowledge Bookstore family, Sean and Carolette Liburd and Michele Liburd. Thank you for letting me live at your store (literally). Walking down from my apartment to access so many books about African culture and history has motivated my life incredibly. Thank you for the support of my artistic endeavours and for creating a space in Brampton where we could learn about and express ourselves.